Rune Marked

Dragons of Isentol Book 2

RICHARD FIERCE

and

pdmac

Cover design by germancreative.

Cover art by Rosauro Ugang

ISBN: 978-1-947329-46-1

THANK YOU

To our wives, with all our hearts

Contents

CHAPTER 1

Gwen

Gwen could smell rain in the air.

Her mount's ears perked up as thunder rumbled ominously overhead, but otherwise, the animal continued trudging along the road undeterred. Aimil rode next to Gwen, her attention focused ahead.

"Should we try to find shelter?" Gwen asked.

Aimil shrugged. "A little rain never hurt anyone."

Gwen decided that was a fair point, but she didn't find the idea of getting soaked very appealing. Since she had no idea how to get to their destination, she was left with no other choice but to continue following Aimil.

The rain started as a gentle sprinkle and quickly turned into a downpour. The road was worn from wagon traffic and the indents left from the wheels quickly filled with water, tinted brown from the dirt.

Between the storms and the complete lack of civilization, Gwen was glad to have Aimil's company over the last few days. The woman had her quiet moments, but she never shied away from conversation. Any time Gwen started to think about her father or Tobias, she would divert her mind by asking Aimil a random question. If Aimil had grown tired of her, she did well to hide it.

They rode through the storm and the sun eventually returned, making the air feel thick and humid. Gwen's wet clothes stuck to her skin, irritating her and making her mutter foul curses under her breath. The two traveled a half-mile after the last of the rain fell before Gwen spotted a town ahead. A poorly made sign displayed the town's name: Woodpine.

"Have you been here before?" Gwen asked.

"I usually pass through without stopping. There's not much to see."

Gwen frowned in disappointment. Aimil hadn't set a breakneck pace by any means, but it was steady with few stops. Unless she had to relieve herself, Aimil barely left the saddle. As the road led them into the heart of Woodpine, Gwen found the place similar to Dawsbury. They even had an inn, which made Gwen question what Aimil meant when she said there wasn't much to see. There was always something interesting to see at an inn.

Aimil continued through the town without stopping and as they were about to cross over a small bridge, a group of armed men stepped into the road in front of them. They wore piecemeal armor and their weapons were more rust than metal.

"Halt!" One of the men shouted, pointing a spear at Aimil's horse.

Gwen pulled on the reigns, forcing her mount to stop. Aimil continued ahead until the spear tip was inches from her horse before she directed the animal to stop. The man with the spear seemed uncertain and glanced around at his fellows.

"What's the issue?" Aimil asked.

"You've got to pay the toll," the man with the spear said.

"Yeah, pay the toll!" Another chimed in.

"Are you in service to the king of Steepcross?"

"Bah! The king is a fool," the spearman replied. "He's off in his castle ignoring all the problems around here. So, you know what we said? We said, 'we're going to make our own laws.' And one of those laws is you have to pay a toll to cross this bridge."

"And if I don't want to pay the toll?" Aimil asked calmly.

"Then we'll take it from you by force," one of the other men threatened.

"Move out of my way," Aimil said.

The group of brigands exchanged looks and whispers with each other, and Gwen assumed that they must not have received a reaction like Aimil's before. They seemed confused about how to handle Aimil. Finally, the spearman poked the horse and said, "Pay first, then we'll move."

Aimil looked at Gwen, then back at the brigands. Gwen saw the look in Aimil's eyes and guessed trouble was going to ensue. She was about to turn her horse around when Aimil lifted her left arm and said, "*Tine!*"

Flames erupted from her hand, catching the spear on fire and causing the group of men to stagger back from the heat. The apparent leader dropped the spear and threw his hands up in defeat.

"I don't like repeating myself," Aimil said.

"No need to," the man said hurriedly. "Let's go, boys. Clear the way!"

The brigands dispersed from the road and Aimil flicked her reigns. Her mount continued along the road and Gwen urged her horse to follow. As they crossed the bridge, Gwen thought she could hear someone crying out for help. There was a shack on the left, old and dilapidated. She guessed the sound was coming from there.

"Do you hear that?" Gwen asked.

"It's probably a trap," Aimil replied.

"Maybe, but what if it's not?"

Aimil stopped her horse and turned her gaze on Gwen. "If it is, are you prepared to have the blood of these fools on your hands? We can easily leave right now, but if it's a trap and we have to fight our way out, these men will die. Swords and spears cannot overpower magic."

Gwen hesitated. The cry for help sounded genuine. She couldn't leave knowing someone might need help, but the thought of killing the brigands didn't sit well with her, either.

"I think we should check it out."

"Suit yourself," Aimil said. She dismounted and headed for the shack. Gwen slid out of the saddle and jogged to catch up. The brigands watched them until Aimil opened the door of the shack. The leader stalked toward them.

"Stop!" He shouted. "Don't go in there!"

Aimil ignored him and stepped inside. Gwen peeked through the doorway curiously, but she kept her focus on the men around them. Gwen lifted her arm, facing her palm at the approaching leader. He stopped in his tracks, but his expression revealed his anger. Aimil stepped out a moment later, followed by a young elf.

Despite his disheveled look and dirty clothes, Gwen thought there was something regal about the elf. His blond hair was matted and a smear of blood ran the length of his forehead. Twin pools of emerald green stared at Gwen and she averted her gaze, somehow feeling inferior.

"That's our elf," the brigand leader said.

"Says who?" Aimil questioned.

"Says me. We captured him fair and square. You aren't stealing our reward."

"Reward?" Gwen asked. "What do you mean?"

"That elf is the prince of Auleavell. He ran off and his father is offering a reward to anyone who returns him. Me and my boys are going to do just that."

"No, I don't think so," Aimil said. "He's coming with us."

"Are you deaf, woman? I just said you aren't stealing our reward."

"How much is the elven king offering?"

"A thousand gold astrals."

"How about a wave of flames and death instead?" Aimil asked.

The leader's bravado disappeared and he spat on the ground. "Blasted mage," he grunted.

"He'll ride with me," Aimil told Gwen, then she walked back to where they'd left the horses. The brigands eyed them with hatred, but none of them were brave enough to risk testing Aimil's promise of death.

Gwen mounted her horse and waited for Aimil to take the lead. She continuously looked over her shoulder to make sure the men weren't doing anything. Aimil's horse began trotting along and Gwen urged her mount into motion. They put a decent distance between them and Woodpine, then Aimil guided her horse to the left, off the road. They rode into a thicket of trees and Aimil dismounted, trying her reigns to a tree branch.

"What are we doing?" Gwen asked. "It's still daylight."

"I want to make sure those fools don't do anything stupid," Aimil replied. "The last thing we need is to be surprised in the middle of the night."

"Good point," Gwen said, dismounting and tying her horse next to Aimil's.

The elf they'd rescued was subdued. He sat down on the ground among the trees. His eyes moved back and forth from Gwen to Aimil.

"Let me guess," he said. "You're going to take me back to my father and take his money."

"Possibly," Aimil replied. "Then again, maybe not. What are you doing out here, anyway?"

"I left my father's court willingly," he answered. "His closed view of the world around us is suffocating, at best. I've heard the gossip among my father's servants. King Torian is threatening our peaceful way of life. My father doesn't believe Torian is a menace, so he's ignoring the rebellion's pleas for help. I refuse to stand with my father on this."

"So, you ran off to a human kingdom?" Aimil asked. "You do know Auleavell and Steepcross aren't exactly on friendly terms, right?"

"I know that," the elf said. "I'm not a fool. I was on my way to Isentol to find the rebellion when those humans attacked me. Attacked me! Within Auleavell's borders, no less. How they managed to get past our patrols is a mystery that's been plaguing me for days."

"Well, it seems you are in luck," Gwen said. "Aimil and I are part of the rebellion against King Torian."

"Truly? Oh, thank the goddess. I was afraid I had traded one captor for another."

"What's your name?" Gwen asked.

"Kirith of House Euldin."

"Well, Kirith, it seems your friends aren't quite ready to give up on that reward," Aimil said. "Stay low."

Gwen hid behind a large tree and peered around the edge. The brigands they'd left behind were coming up the road swiftly, all of them riding horses. Gwen guessed they had stolen them from the people of Woodpine.

The leader slowed his mount and whistled, pointing toward the thicket where Gwen and her companions were hiding.

"The tracks go that way," he said.

Gwen watched the men dismount and draw their weapons. She looked at Aimil. The woman had turned her attention behind them. She tilted her head to the side, listening to something Gwen couldn't hear.

"What is it?" Gwen whispered harshly.

Aimil held up her finger, a sign for Gwen to be quiet. Kirith's head jerked to the side and his eyes widened.

"Sentinels are coming!" he warned.

Aimil cursed and beckoned Gwen to come closer. The two women rushed to where Kirith was and Aimil closed her eyes. A moment later, one of the runes on her right arm began to glow with a sickly green light.

"Don't move," Aimil said softly. "I can hide us visibly, but noise can still be heard."

Gwen stood completely still. She didn't realize she was holding her breath until she started to hear her heart beating in her ears.

Kirith slowly lifted a hand and pointed. Gwen looked and didn't see anything at first, but then she saw movement. It was almost imperceptible. A tall elf wearing leather armor that mirrored his surroundings slipped through the thicket without a sound. He carried a bow in one hand and a quiver of arrows across his back.

The elf stopped when he spotted the brigands and raised his bow, slipping an arrow onto the string. He took aim and paused. Gwen wondered what he was waiting on, but then she spotted more movement. Three other elves, similarly dressed as the first, moved into position and readied their arrows.

At an unspoken command, the elves let their arrows fly at the same time. Each arrow struck a target, taking down half the group of brigands. The leader shouted a retreat, but the elven sentinels fired off another round of projectiles to finish the job.

Gwen swallowed hard and hoped the elves would disappear as quickly as they returned. Kirith closed his eyes and lowered his head into his hands. The elves investigated the bodies of the brigands and then left in the direction they'd come. Gwen looked at Aimil. The woman had her eyes open now, and she was watching the trees intently.

"Are they gone?" Gwen whispered.

An arrow whizzed past her face, so close she felt the wind stir against her lips. She jerked her head back belatedly in surprise and noticed an elf standing behind Aimil. She pointed wordlessly, her eyes widened in terror. The elf pressed the tip of a sword to Aimil's back.

"Tell me why I shouldn't end your life," the elf demanded.

CHAPTER 2

Conal

One hand on top of the other, resting on the pommel of his saddle, Conal sat astride his steed on the crest of the road, staring at the city of Hemlin in the near distance, remembering the last time he was here. "Are you sure we have to go in there?"

"We need a place to rest," Bryok reminded him. "Besides, you're a different person than the last time you were here." He flicked his reins, urging his mount forward.

Conal ticked his head at the city. "Tell that to them."

"I'm hungry," Torgreth said, squeezing the flanks of his stout pony.

"Why'd we come this way when we're supposed to be heading to Denhelm," Conal complained, catching up to ride beside the dwarf.

"Like I've already said… several times," Bryok answered with a hint of frustration, "we need to meet with someone here." He scanned the road and the surrounding farmland. All seemed normal with the usual traffic headed in and out of the city gates.

"Who is this guy again?" Conal asked.

"He's a friend. He's the one who told me about you."

Conal raised an eyebrow in doubt. "If you knew about me, why didn't you come get me, *before* I got branded?"

Bryok paused then said, "Because there were other matters that demanded my attention."

"Like what?"

Bryok cast a glance at Torgreth. "Like two dwarves that needed immediate rescuing."

"Yer brother scared the piss out of us," Torgreth chuckled.

"Drustan can be intense at times."

"Ya think?" Conal snorted a laugh.

Merging into the ebb and flow of travelers, farmers, clerics, and merchants, Conal was surprised when the two guards at the gate paid them scant attention. "Something's not right," he quietly commented as they passed through the gatehouse. "They didn't even make eye contact."

"Maybe they're bored," Torgreth offered.

"They weren't bored the last time I was here," Conal countered. It wasn't until they were halfway up the main street towards the market square that he blurted, "They're not real guards."

"What?" Bryok and Torgreth replied in unison.

"They're not real guards," Conal repeated, spinning around. "Look at the uniforms. They're wearing the red jackets, but where's the rest of the uniform? The boots? The helmet?"

Bryok paused to cast a concerned glance over his shoulder. "We need to find my friend. Find out what's going on. Follow me."

Bryok set a brisk pace, taking streets and alleyways around the market square to the stables. Once their mounts were settled, Bryok led them deeper into the back alleys of the city. At the corner of one alleyway, Conal grabbed his two companions' arms and dragged the into the shadows.

"Wha –" Torgreth began before Conal jabbed a finger to his lips and pointed across the street to a man pretending to be nonchalant, leaning against the wall by a residence door as he studied the passersby.

"That's Jestyn. Oscon has to be close by." Conal's sudden desire for revenge bubbled up as he silently deliberated how.

"Leave him," Bryok urged. "We'll deal with him later. We need to find my friend."

"I'm not going until I see what he's up to."

"We don't have time for this," Bryok fussed. "We'll come back for him."

Ignoring him, Conal lifted a foot to step out when the door opened and Oscon emerged, blinking in the sunlight. "There you are," Conal snarled.

He was halfway across the street before anyone realized. Jestyn was the first to see him.

"Well look who's back," he mocked until he saw the grim determination in Conal's eyes. Immediately interspersing himself between his boss and the approaching former highwayman, he placed a hand on the handle of the dagger by his side, a warning that he would not hesitate to use it. Remembering the young man's past with the highwaymen, he was neither intimidated nor worried that he could handle this young pup.

"Hold it right there," Jestyn ordered, a hand pressed forward.

Conal stared past Jestyn to see the smirk plastered on Oscon's face, a smirk that said he would repeat Conal's humiliation if necessary.

Oscon's arrogance grew when Jestyn slipped the blade out and pointed it at Conal. His smirk abruptly vanished when Conal smacked the blade out of Jestyn's hand then delivered such a blow to the man's chest that it cracked several ribs and sent him flying backwards to crash against the stonewalls of the building only to crumple into a heap on the street.

What followed next happened so fast that Oscon wasn't quite sure how he ended up with Conal's hand wrapped around his throat, his body lifted inches off the ground. What he did know was the vice-grip squeezing his throat hurt and he couldn't breathe. In desperation, he grabbed the dagger in his boot and swung up to stab Conal in the gut, only to have his thrust stopped short, Conal's grip so tight that he felt his hand grow numb, the blade slipping from his fingers to rattle on the ground.

"You set me up," Conal growled, his anger adding power to his strength. "You condemned me to be a slave."

He felt a calm hand touch his arm and heard Bryok say, "Let's not kill him quite yet. We still need information from him."

"C'mon Conal," Torgreth urged when Conal hesitated. "You can kill him later. I'll even help if you want. We can cut off his fingers then his toes, peel his eyelids off and even cut out his tongue."

Startled at the gruesome details, Conal twisted his head to gaze at the dwarf who returned his look with a loopy grin. "You are one strange dwarf," he chuckled, shaking his head.

"Mama said the same thing about me." Torgreth's grin widened.

Conal relaxed his grip and Oscon sucked in a deep breath.

Bryok stared down at Oscon. "You're coming with us. You make one false move and you're a dead man."

"What about him?" Torgreth hooked a thumb at Jestyn who hadn't moved, his hands clutching his ribs.

"Leave him," Bryok answered. "Doubt he'll be going very far anytime soon."

Torgreth bent down and picked up Oscon's dagger, twisting it around in his hands. "Nice dagger. Where'd you get it?"

Oscon shifted a wary glance at them, his hand rubbing his throat. "Bought it a while ago."

"Really?" Torgreth shot him a 'you're a liar' look. He held up the dagger so that his two friends could see. "This dagger is made from dwarven iron. The smith's mark is here." He pointed to a symbol beneath the quillon. "Note the crown in the mark? The maker was a king's smithy." He turned to give Oscon a hard stare. "There hasn't been a king's smithy in any dwarven land for over 150 years."

"How do you know that?" Conal asked, impressed.

"Because the last king's smithy was Gunnar Iron-hammer. He was my grandfather." Narrowing his stare at the man, his lip curled in anger. "I'll ask you once more. Where did you get it?"

Oscon looked down upon the dwarf, shrugging in feigned ignorance.

Torgreth turned to Bryok. "Can I kill him?"

"Not yet," Bryok answered with a curious frown. "What more can you tell us of the blade?"

"It was most likely a gift from my grandfather to the king in Isentol."

"Kamron?" Conal blurted.

"No, my young friend," Torgreth answered with an indulgent smile. "It would have been King Cered, Kamron's great-great grandfather." He turned back to Bryok. "This is a king's gift, which means it is also probably elven imbued." He twisted his head to give Oscon a look of disdain. "And this fool probably didn't even know it."

"Elven imbued?" Conal marveled before a curtain pulled back from nearby window diverted his focus and he suddenly noticed passersby slowing their stride to gawk. "We're beginning to draw attention."

Torgreth jabbed the dagger point into Oscon's side. "Start walking. Pray that I don't accidently stumble and stick this all the way in."

Oscon's arrogance returned as he moved away from the door and into the street. Catching Jestyn's eye, he ticked his head in a quick nod, receiving a nod of understanding in return. "You fools. You don't know who yer messin' with. When word gets out what you done, yer lives won't be worth a copper royal."

Conal noted the exchange between the two outlaws and calmly walked over to Jestyn who had struggled to his knees. Grabbing him by his shirt, he effortlessly lifted him up to dangle above the street.

"Don't think I've forgotten your part in all this. When I'm finished with Oscon, I'm coming for you. I will make you suffer like never before. Tell the rest of them. I'm coming for them too. You all betrayed me. I don't care where you run. I will find you."

His anger growing, Conal spun around, Jestyn whirling like a rag doll, and flung his former associate against the stone wall. Jestyn flopped to the ground, his arm broken.

Leaving Jestyn groaning in pain, Conal twisted his head to glare at the passersby who quickly gave urgency to their steps.

"My, my," Oscon sneered with false bravura, "such violence. Pity I didn't know this about you before. I can use a man like you."

"We need to go," Bryok intervened.

Leading the way, Bryok led them through streets and back alleys as they moved single file, with Oscon behind Bryok, Torgreth behind Oscon, the dagger's blade firm against the man's side, and Conal bringing up the rear. At one nondescript door halfway down a deserted alley, Bryok stopped and knocked in a rhythmic pattern of three-two-three-one knocks. A peephole door slid to the side.

Bryok leaned forward and whispered, "Dragon home."

The peephole door closed, and the heavy oak door silently swung open revealing a hulking brute of a man whose intimidating scowl reminded those attempting to force their way in that he would personally inflict mayhem on them.

"Is he here?" Bryok asked.

The man nodded and lifted a thick arm to point down the darkened corridor.

By the tine Conal entered, Bryok was hallway down the hall. The door closed behind him and he squinted to see light coming from beneath the door at the end of the hall. Light spilled out into the corridor when Bryok opened the door then stood to the side as the others stepped into a large room sparsely furnished whose sole occupant stood close to the fireplace, reading a book on a tall book stand. Wall sconces surrounding the room provided more than ample light.

Conal startled for the tall individual behind the book stand was an elf.

"Greetings, Galadyr," Bryok said with a respectful nod.

"Greetings, my friend," the elf replied with a warm smile, closing the book. Galadyr stood a little taller than Conal. He wore a sleeveless tunic of supple forest brown leather, and woolen breeches the color of faded crimson, tucked into stout leather boots that ended just below his knees. His long blond hair was held back by a braided leather cord wrapped around his forehead revealing the telltale pointed ears.

"This one," Bryok indicated Oscon, "needs guarding."

No sooner had he finished that the door opened and the hulking man at the outside door stepped in.

"Take that one," Galadyr said, pointing a slender finger at Oscon, "and see that he is well contained."

"What's going on?" Oscon demanded. "You can't treat me like this."

The hulking man growled and went to reach for Oscon.

"Easy Brunet," Galadyr soothed before addressing Oscon. "You have a choice on how you can leave this room. Choose wisely."

Oscon's eyes twitched from Brunet to Conal to the elf, knowing he had only one choice. Snarling, he jerked around to follow Brunet.

Once the door closed behind them, Galadyr shifted his devoted attention to Conal. "Is this he?"

"Yes," Bryok answered. "What's going on in the city? Who is guarding the gates?"

"There has been some unrest," Galadyr explained. "The men you saw were new recruits. They have not had time to be fully kitted."

"Unrest?"

"Rumors mostly… enough to make Pharyl exercise caution."

Accepting the answer, he nodded for Torgreth to show Galadyr the dagger. "There is also this."

"Well met, friend Torgreth," the elf greeted him, accepting the dagger. "The reasons for your escape have been made known to me."

"And who are you?" the dwarf boldly asked.

Galadyr raised a finger telling him to wait while he studied the dagger. "This is a king's dagger." Holding the dagger in both hands, he bent his head and closed his eyes, bringing the flat of the blade up and pressing it against his forehead. A thick silence filled the room as they waited and watched Galadyr's serene face morph to a heavy frown. Opening his eyes, he inhaled a slow breath.

"The dagger's name is 'Bloodthirst.'" He tilted his head to stare at Torgreth, his cobalt blues eyes boring into him. "Where did you find this?"

"Oscon had it," Torgreth replied. "It's elven imbued, isn't it."

"Yes," Galadyr nodded, shifting his gaze to Bryok. "I will question the other in a bit. We must discern how he came by this."

"What's so special about it?" Conal asked.

"It is a king's dagger," Galadyr explained.

"Everyone keeps saying that," Conal interrupted.

"A king's dagger," Galadyr patiently continued, "can only be forged by a dwarf, and not just any dwarf." He tilted his head to narrow his gaze at Torgreth. "The dwarf must be from the lineage of the Iron Hand, like you. Once the dagger is crafted, it is carried to the eleven kingdom of Auleavell where mages imbue the blade with a special gift. Some are warning blades that glow or hum when danger is near. Others are reactive blades that give additional strength to the man who wields it so that if attacked, he can defeat his enemies. Still others, like Bloodthirst here, were designed to wreak vengeance, thirsting for blood and death until the threat is no more. It is a blade to be fearful of, because in the wrong hands it can do much damage."

Conal's brow furrowed. "Then why didn't Oscon have this power?"

Galadyr looked at him as thought the answer obvious. "He is not a king."

"So only a king can use this dagger?"

"A king or one descended from a king."

Conal blinked at the revelation. "May I see it?"

Ignoring Bryok's look of fear, Galadyr handed him the dagger.

Grasping the handle, Conal felt a sudden surge of rage fill his entire body as the clarity of the room clouded so that only the dagger had any visible form. The blade in his hands felt like an extension of his own body and his head snapped up and the cloud vanished as his angry eyes locked on each one in the room, instantaneously measuring each individual's threat towards him. Then just as suddenly, the seething storm disappeared and he stood in the middle of the room, his heart pounding as though coming off the battlefield.

"What did you see?" Galadyr held his hand out for the dagger.

"I didn't see anything," he replied, catching his breath, reluctant to surrender the blade.

"What did you feel?" Galadyr fixed him with a firm stare, his hand still out.

With a disappointed sigh, he handed the dagger to him. "I felt anger, totally consuming anger, like I wanted to kill everything around me. But then when I looked at each of you, the anger went away."

"That's because we were not a threat to you." Galadyr slid a satisfied glance at Bryok.

"I have a question," Torgreth announced, looking straight at Galadyr. "Who are you?"

"I am Galadyr."

"Yeah, we know. Where are you from? Why are you here?" Torgreth folded his arms across his chest.

Galadyr paused as if deliberating how much to tell. "I am from Auleavell."

"Long way from home," Torgreth observed.

"Yes, that is true." Studying the dwarf then Conal, he placed the dagger on top of the book he was reading and cupped his hands behind his back. "I am a friend of Prince Kirith."

"Who's he?"

"Let him finish," Bryok chided.

"Sorry," Torgreth lamely replied.

"Prince Kirith," Galadyr continued, "is King Falael's son, one of the few who recognizes and understands the threat the kingdom faces."

Torgreth was about to say 'so you ran away' when reminded of his own flight from Havyrd and King

Rorykn. Instead he said, "So you came here to look for help?"

"Yes, which leads me to ask how that fellow came by this dagger. Its original home was in Havengarde. How did it end up here? I think it's time we found out."

"He's not gonna say much," Torgreth warned. "We tried already."

Galadyr smiled. "I'm sure you have. Let's try again." He held up the dagger and cast a sly glance at Conal. "Perhaps I should give this to you when we interrogate him."

CHAPTER 3

Gwen

Gwen and Aimil marched wordlessly between the elven sentinels, their hands bound behind their backs with silken cord. Kirith wasn't bound, but the leader of the sentinels kept a close eye on him. Gwen knew that they had been traveling along the border between Auleavell and Steepcross, but she hadn't expected to stumble upon a group of elven soldiers, let alone their prince.

The Aspect of all the elves glowed green. Gwen remembered that Eradore had said that she would get accustomed to seeing them and he'd been right. It was there in the background, an incorporeal *thing*, but she didn't really notice it unless she focused on it. Aimil's was blue, like her own, and she unexpectedly remembered the dwarf from the attack on the outpost. His Aspect had been brown.

"Release them," Kirith said. It was a litany from him, repeated every so often.

"I cannot, my Lord," the lead sentinel answered, just as he had every other time.

Gwen found the sentinel armor intriguing. It was enchanted with magic, that much was obvious to her. The material was constantly changing to mirror the scenery around them, cloaking the elves in perfect camouflage.

"Am I not the prince of Auleavell?" Kirith asked. "Or has my father taken that as well?"

"You are still the prince, my Lord."

"Then why will you not heed my command to let them go?"

The leader remained silent.

"Blast you, Haladavar!"

Gwen repeated the name under her breath. It rolled off her tongue like honey. She looked at Aimil. The woman had been silent since they'd been captured, and she wore a scowl plastered across her face.

"I'm sorry I got you into this," Gwen said.

"Don't be," Aimil replied. "If I didn't want to be here, do you really think these ropes would stop me?"

Gwen had been wondering about that. She'd considered using her lightning against the sentinels, but since Eradore had asked her to deliver a message to someone in Auleavell, she didn't think that was the best idea. Apparently neither did Aimil.

"Then why do you look so angry?"

"Angry?" Aimil laughed. "This is my normal face out in the world. It keeps people from bothering me."

"Silence!" Haladavar snapped, looking over his shoulder at them.

Gwen glared at him but she didn't speak another word. They trekked through thick woodland for several hours and Gwen could feel blisters forming on the bottoms of her feet. Her throat was dry and all she wanted was to sit long enough for the ache in her legs to go away. She staggered a few times, almost tripping over tree roots. The air grew less humid the further they traveled, which Gwen was thankful for.

The sound of civilization drew Gwen's attention and she perked up, looking ahead for the source of the noises. Numerous trees, many of them as thick as buildings, towered over the rest of the forest. Elegant archways were carved into their facades, providing natural entrances to the interior of the trees. Gwen's breath caught in her throat at the staggering beauty.

"There's nothing like it anywhere else," Aimil whispered. "And I've traveled to many places."

Standing outside some of the trees, guards holding spears and polearms watched everyone with an eye of suspicion. As Gwen and the others traversed the main path through the city, some of the elves looked at them distrustfully and others outright ignored their presence. Gwen noticed the tension among the elves and wondered what had happened recently.

Haladavar led them to the largest tree Gwen had ever seen. Its trunk was wide enough to hold six carriages end to end. It rose into the sky, the canopy lost high above. Gwen stopped walking as she admired the tree. The guard behind her shoved her roughly and she fell to her knees with a grunt. Kirith turned around and glared at the guard, then helped Gwen to her feet.

"I'm sorry," he said quietly. "I will right this wrong."

They continued into the massive tree and Gwen's mind spun at the intricate details that had been carved into the walls. Stags, unicorns, and odd symbols and shapes covered every inch of space. The area they entered was a large open assembly room with two winding stairways on either side that led up to the next level.

"Wait here with them," Haladavar told the other guards, then he went up one of the stairways.

Gwen continued to admire the beauty around her until Haladavar appeared at the top of the stairs.

"Bring them!" His voice drifted down to them, filled with authority.

The guards prodded Gwen and Aimil, and the two climbed the ornate staircase. When they reached the top, Haladavar led them past an open balcony that offered a magnificent view of the forest-city, then up a smaller set of stairs. An ivory throne wrapped in vines sat against the back wall. Falael, king of Auleavell, sat in the throne, his hard eyes fixed on Kirith.

Two guards stood at either side of the king, armed and intimidating. Gwen found their demeanor so different from Eradore's.

"The lamb returns to the fold," Falael said. His eyes roamed the rest of the group and his attention paused on Gwen and Aimil, then he looked questioningly at Haladavar. "Why are there humans in my kingdom?"

"These are the people we found Prince Kirith with, my Lord."

"A fact you neglected in your report moments ago."

"My apologies," Haladavar said, bowing his head.

"Forgiven," Falael said. He looked back at Kirith. "Tell me, is my fist so iron-shod that you can't bear the weight of living under it?"

"I left because you refuse to see the threat that lies before all of us," Kirith replied. "King Torian is trying to expand his kingdom and he will stop at nothing until he rules every inch of land."

"Is that so? How would you know this? Have you been to Isentol?"

"No," Kirith answered.

"Do you see King Torian's armies at our doorstep?"

"No," Kirith repeated.

"Then tell me how you know such things without signs of proof?"

Kirith bowed his head in defeat.

"Lyra has come here and poisoned the minds of our young generations. She spews lies and deceit about our neighbor with no proof. This is why she has been removed from my court."

Gwen perked up at the mention of Lyra's name. That was the person that Gwen needed to deliver a message to. She glanced at Aimil. The woman shook her head ever so slightly. Gwen wanted to ask the king where Lyra was, but her exhaustion took away her will.

"We need to find Lyra," Gwen whispered.

"We'll worry about that later. We have bigger problems right now."

"What problems?"

"Why do these humans speak in my presence without permission?" Falael demanded.

"I'm sorry," Gwen said loudly. "I meant no offense."

"And yet, like a wild dog, she continues to bay. Are these the humans you saw within our borders?"

"Possibly," Haladavar replied. "We did kill some others that were armed."

"Trespassing in Auleavell is strictly prohibited," Falael said.

"They weren't trespassing," Kirith spoke up. "They rescued me from the ones who captured me."

"A human doing a just deed? I find it difficult to believe." Falael looked at Haladavar, who frowned.

"You dispel the rumors of King Torian's ill intent, yet you claim that humans are incapable of doing what is just? Do you not see your own madness?" Kirith asked.

"The poison in his mind seeps from his mouth," Falael said. "Take the humans away. Their trial will be held in the morning."

Kirith tried to protest, but Falael shot him a glare, silencing him. One of the guards grabbed ahold of Gwen's arm roughly and snapped a thin bracelet around her wrist. The faint pulse of magic that was always within her suddenly disappeared. She turned to Aimil in shock, her eyes widening.

Aimil jerked away from the guard trying to grab her and struck a blow to the side of his face. The elf collapsed in an unconscious heap, but another took his place. Aimil backstepped and lifted her right hand. Gwen winced, preparing for the flare of magic, but it never came. She opened her eyes to see Aimil frozen in place. She looked around, but no one else was affected.

"Must I do everything myself?" Falael asked. He was standing now, his left hand held out in front of him, fingers splayed wide. The other guards hurriedly snapped several bracelets onto Aimil's wrists and then Falael released his spell.

Gwen guessed by the look on Aimil's face that she was trying to use her runes, but nothing was happening. "What is this?" she growled.

"It is for your safety, as well as ours," Falael answered. "Now get them out of my sight. And take Prince Kirith as well. If he wants to wallow in the poison, let him."

Haladavar motioned the other guards to follow him and he escorted them up higher into the tree. Gwen looked back at the fallen elf, hoping Aimil hadn't killed him. Just as he was leaving her line of sight, she saw him sit up. She sighed in relief, but was anxious about where they were headed. If Falael had such a dim view of humans, she assumed they were going to be taken to a nightmare of a prison.

As it turned out, the 'prison' was an extremely comfortable room with an open view of the forest-city. Gwen looked around, assuming that the room must be for Kirith. Since he was a prince, he'd be well taken care of. Yet as Haladavar left all three of them inside, she was glad to be proven wrong. The other guards closed the doors and barred them from the outside.

"So these trees do have doors," Aimil said.

"Only the personal chambers," Kirith replied. "This is a guest room for visiting nobles."

"And your father expects us to stay here all night, just to face a trial tomorrow?" Gwen asked.

"Sadly, yes. My father is a difficult man, as you have seen."

"No wonder you ran away," Aimil said. She pulled at the bracelets, but they didn't budge. "What are these blasted things?"

"Those are shackles. They will keep you from leaving the boundaries of the city by force of pain."

"They are also cutting off my magic," Aimil huffed. "How do I get them off?"

"Yes, they do restrict magic. Only the guards can remove them."

Aimil growled in frustration and began pacing back and forth across the room. She reminded Gwen of a wild animal. The woman couldn't handle being caged.

"What is this trial your father mentioned?" Gwen asked.

"He thinks you've trespassed into Auleavell. He closed our borders, which makes your presence here a crime. Tomorrow morning, he'll parade you before the nobles and they will judge whether you are innocent or not."

"There's a chance we'll be declared innocent?"

"That's highly unlikely," Kirith replied. "Many of the nobles share the same limited perspective as my father. They will find you guilty."

"What happens if they think we're guilty?"

"You'll be executed."

Gwen slumped into a nearby chair, exhausted and overwhelmed. Aimil was still pacing. Kirith sat across from Gwen, his expression downcast. That was another difference she noticed among the elves. Kirith was like

Eradore, letting his emotions show on his face. Falael and the guards seemed emotionless, their hearts hard.

"Your father mentioned someone named Lyra. Do you know her?"

"Yes," Kirith replied. "She is a voice of reason among my people. Lyra has opened my eyes to the threat that Torian poses."

"I have a message for her from a friend." Gwen didn't necessarily consider Eradore a friend, but she wasn't sure what else to call him. Her leader? That didn't sound right, either.

"My father banished her from the court," Kirith said.

"What does that mean?"

"She's not permitted inside this tree, but she is allowed to stay in the city."

"Do you know where to find her?" Aimil asked, walking over to join them.

"There are a few places she could be, but what does it matter?"

"It matters because we're going to sneak out of here."

"How do you propose that?" Kirith asked. "You have no magic and my father has guards at the door."

"We're not going out of the door," Aimil replied. She looked away and Gwen followed her gaze to the open balcony.

"We're going out that way."

CHAPTER 4

Conal

Oscon was tied to a chair when they entered the room, one eye swollen, surrounded by a purple bruise. Dried blood edged the corner of his lips.

"What happened?" Conal asked, amused at the change in the man's fortune.

"He was being uncooperative," Brunet replied with an unemotional shrug.

Oscon bent his head up to glare at them. "Yer wasting my time. I got nuthin' to say to you."

"Yes," Galadyr blithely replied, "we know. That's why we're going to let Conal torture you." He handed a set of iron pliers to Conal.

Conal looked over at Torgreth, furrowing his brow. "How did that go again? We cut off his fingers then his toes, peel his eyelids off then cut out his tongue?"

"Something like that." Torgreth grinned at Oscon. "This is gonna be fun. You're not going to enjoy it, but we will."

"Yer bluffing," Oscon snarled before turning his venom at Conal. "I shoulda dumped you long ago. You were nuthin' but a dead weight, good fer nuthin'. That's why I got rid of you."

Conal stood before him, pliers in hand. "That's the best you got? Let's see if you sing the same tune." He pulled up his sleeve to reveal his brand. "Recognize that?"

Oscon's defiance wavered. "What the hell? You're a Cobra?"

"You've got eyes. What does it look like?"

"But… when did that happen?"

"I've been one all along," Conal lied. "You think I didn't know you were working for Caldyr? That you were also sending reports back to Havengarde? Why do you think I joined your band of fools? Because I was so impressed with your leadership?" He barked a derisive laugh. "Puh-lease."

"You gonna talk him to death," Torgreth interrupted, "or are we gonna get to torturing?"

"You're right," Conal said with a smile, squeezing the pliers several times. "The one thing I couldn't discover before my untimely departure was who your contact was. Let's start with the fingernails." He grabbed Oscon's hand and pried a finger back, jamming the pliers against the fingertip and clamping down on the fingernail.

"Wait a minute," Bryok intervened. "If you're going to torture him, what's the incentive for him to tell you anything?"

Conal frowned, pondering the question then shrugged. "I was more curious than anything else. I didn't think he'd tell us. Just though I'd ask before we began."

"Suppose he agrees to tell us what we need to know?" Bryok ventured. "Do we need to torture him?"

"You mean not torture him if he tells us what we need to know?" Conal stared at him like he was spoiling all his fun.

"That was the general idea."

Conal shifted a look to Oscon then back to Bryok. "How do we know he's telling the truth?"

"We don't."

"Then what does it matter what he says? Let's just get on with it." He started tugging on the fingernail. "Wonder which hurts more, just yanking it out or tugging slowly?"

"Pain lasts longer if you tug it slowly," Torgreth observed.

Oscon tensed, struggling to disengage his finger from Conal's vice grip. Sweat dripped down his temples and forehead.

"Before you rip that out," Bryok pointed out, "we still haven't determined where he got the dagger."

"Ah, that's right. I did ask, didn't I. Still, like I said, what does it matter? But... just to humor you, I'll play along." Conal relaxed the pressure just a bit then started tugging again, locking his gaze on Oscon. "You want to tell us about the dagger?" He tugged harder.

"Blayne gave it to me," he bellowed.

"Blayne? As in Brody's son Blayne?"

"Yes, yes. He gave it to me."

"Where did he get it?"

"I don't know. I swear it. I don't know."

"Really?" Conal tugged harder.

"O god, I swear."

"Was Brody your contact?"

"Yes, yes."

"He's lying," Torgreth sneered. "Yank it out."

"O god, O god, please. I swear it's the truth."

Conal slid a glance at Galadyr who dipped his head in a quick nod. The door opened and a man slipped in, pretending to whisper something in Galadyr's ear.

"We'll need to continue this later," Galadyr announced.

Without a word, they slipped out the room, leaving Oscon sweating and breathing heavily, his imagination rampant with anticipated pain.

Back in Galadyr's room, Conal chuckled. "That was easier than I expected. For someone who was supposed to be so tough, I barely tugged on his fingernail and he started whining like a little girl."

"You all played your parts very well," Galadyr smiled.

"What do we do with him?" Bryok questioned. "We can't release him, and we can't leave him here."

Galadyr saw Conal's overt look at the dagger. "I don't think that's a good idea."

"What?"

"Remember your experience with it?"

"You afraid I can't control myself?" Conal folded his arms across his chest.

"Yes." Galadyr placed the dagger on the book on the bookstand, his hands resting on top.

"If that belongs to the king, by rights, isn't that mine?"

"You're not a king," Bryok calmly reminded him. "You're the son of a king."

"Huh?" Torgreth burst.

Realizing his indiscretion, Bryok heaved a sigh of irritation at himself. "You might as well know. Conal is King Kamron's son."

"So, it is true," Galadyr intoned.

"You saw for yourself when he handled the blade."

Instead of rejoicing, Galadyr's face tightened. Clasping his hands behind him, he stepped away to begin slowly pacing. "He will need protection."

"Is this joke, another game?" Torgreth demanded.

"It is no joke, Torgreth Iron-hand," Galadyr solemnly replied. "Our friend here is the son of King Kamron."

"How is that even possible?" Torgreth argued. "He was a highwayman and before that lived in some town on the coast." He cast a suspicious eye at Conal.

"It's a surprise to me too," Conal shrugged, "but I'm coming to terms with it."

Torgreth swung his hand in a deep sweeping bow. "My liege."

"Very funny," Conal deadpanned.

Torgreth tilted his head to stare at him. "Aren't you the same guy who jumped out the window and into the river to escape from Drustan?"

"You have to admit it was a good dive," Conal pointed out.

Torgreth smiled then looked up Galadyr. "You wouldn't lie to a dwarf, would you?"

Galadyr smiled despite himself. "No, I wouldn't lie to you. It is true."

"Can we get back to the issue at hand," Bryok chided. "We need to get to Denhelm, and we can't take Oscon with us."

"Why not?" Torgreth asked.

"Because he'll only slow us down."

"And they're probably already looking for him," Conal added before rethinking the problem. "But the longer he stays away, the more likely someone else will take charge... which means his position with his band of followers will have been compromised." A smile curled the corners of his lips. "The longer we can keep him away, the less necessary he becomes, which means my former companions will not want to spend their time looking for us." He shifted his gaze to Galadyr. "Is Brunet coming with us?"

"No. Your idea has merit. We will do as you have suggested."

Bryok narrowed his gaze at Torgreth. "No one else is to know of Conal's true identity, not even your brother."

"I can keep a secret," Torgreth emphatically stated, giving Conal a look that said he was still unsure he wasn't being played.

"We need to leave," Galadyr warned. "Rumors abound that all is not well in Tir Manach. We head for Denhelm and Lord Pharyl as soon as I explain our plan to Brunet."

It was early afternoon when they slipped out the alleyway door and headed to the city gates, stopping by a stable to collect their mounts.

"I'm sure no one will notice us," Conal wryly observed, making his way through the crowded streets, "a dwarf, an elf, and two men... just your everyday group of friends."

"There's nothing we can do about it," Bryok said. "Keep watch for any trouble."

Bryok led the way, Conal beside him, Galadyr and Torgreth behind, Torgreth receiving the most stares. Initially smiling at the overt staring, Torgreth quickly tired of pretending and replaced his smile with a scowl.

"North, north-west," Conal quietly warned. "I recognize the woman. She's one of Oscon's band."

Their eyes met and Conal gave her a smile of recognition, causing surprise and momentary confusion. Abruptly she melted into the swarms of pedestrians.

"She's gone to spread the word about me," Conal said. "We need to hurry."

"Slow down," Bryok countered, reaching for Conal's reins. "We don't need to draw more attention to ourselves."

Finally clearing the city gates, Bryok ordered, "Let's pick up the pace," and spurred his horse to a trot.

"Don't forget about me," Torgreth complained, his pony's rhythm more of a canter than a trot.

"She's a strong mare," Galadyr informed him, "and can keep this pace hours."

"Not sure I can," Torgreth grumbled, struggling to get comfortable in the saddle.

A half mile outside the gate, they crossed the intersection of the road leading north towards Urve and south towards Monkreth. Conal looked back over his shoulder.

"They're coming," he exclaimed.

Nearly twenty riders spilled though the city gates and gave chase. Urging their steeds to a gallop, they knew they could not keep this pace for long. And despite Torgreth's doughty steed, the little pony could not keep pace. Accepting that they could not outrun their pursuers, Bryok slowed their pace to a halt and turned to face the approaching riders who quickly caught up and surrounded them.

A tall man well-built man with a full rust colored beard stepped his horse forward. Leaning forward, he gave Conal a condescending smile. "Hullo Conal,"

"Hello Maldwic." With an indulgent grin, Conal scanned the group. "Sort of makes it hard to keep it a secret that you're all highwaymen when you're so obvious. Which genius thought it was a good idea to ride out all together?"

Maldwic's smug smile wavered as he suddenly realized not only had he compromised the band, but when Oscon found out, his life wasn't worth a copper royal.

"We came to rescue Oscon," he awkwardly said, Oscon's absence painfully obvious.

Conal snorted a laugh. "Let me see if I understand you correctly. You compromised everyone in the company because you wanted to rescue Oscon?" In exaggerated turns of his head, he looked to his left then right. "As you can see, he's not here. Further, wasn't it Oscon himself who said that anyone left behind is on his own? Didn't Oscon say that no one is more important than the company?"

"He's right, Maldwic," a female voice spoke up.

"Seems to me," Conal pointed out, "that if Oscon is on his own, he's no longer the boss anymore. That means someone else has to take his place."

Maldwic's face brightened until Conal added, "Isn't Jestyn next in command.?"

"He ain't here," a male voice said.

Conal cocked his head to the side and narrowed his gaze at Maldwic. "I guess that means you're the boss now."

Momentarily startled at the elevation, Maldwic sat up straight, assuming to role of one in command. "Yer right. I'm the boss now."

"Well, boss," Conal smiled, "what are your plans? Are you going to sit out here where everyone can see you or are you going to fade away and regroup?"

"We're going to regroup," he replied. "Why don't you come with us? I can use a good man like you."

"Much as I'd like to," Conal replied with a feigned sigh, "I'm committed to another venture. Perhaps you might like to join us."

"What're you doing?"

"We're going to Lord Pharyl's to enlist his aid to fight King Torian."

A heavy silence reigned for a moment before Maldwic laughed. "You're a funny one. What're you really doing?"

"It's true," Galadyr spoke up. "We seek alliances to fight against an evil king who, if he is not stopped, will one day rule this very kingdom."

"An elf." Maldwic observed, curling a lip.

"And a half-druid," Conal said, pointing to Bryok.

"And a dwarf," Torgreth chimed in.

There was a visible reaction to the revelation that Conal traveled with a half-druid.

"You travel with interesting companions," Maldwic said, regarding Conal's friends with a wary eye.

"So do you," Conal smiled. "I ask again, will you join us?"

"What's in it for us?"

"Everlasting fame and glory," Conal grandly answered.

Maldwic sniffed a derisive laugh. "Fame and glory don't put food in your belly."

"If that's all you seek, then I can promise that you will have plenty of food."

"We're wastin' time," the female voice scolded.

Conal turned his head to see the speaker, a pretty woman with thick blond hair held back with a leather ringlet. "You're right, Beca. We are wasting time." Addressing Maldwic, he said, "If you're not coming with us, then let us be on our way."

Maldwic frowned then slowly shook his head. "Can't do that."

"Why not?"

"Your friends have seen us."

"They can be trusted," Conal avowed.

"Sez you."

"You're making a huge mistake."

"You're the one making the mistake," Maldwic countered. Before he could command his company to attack, Conal spoke up.

"I challenge you."

"What?"

"I challenge you. By all rights, I'm still part of the company. Because I was captured doesn't change the fact that I am one of you. Even when they tortured me and tried to make me reveal names, I never said a word." Conal was on a roll and his story took on exaggerated proportions. "Even when Oscon set me up, I never said anything. When I was betrayed by my own boss, I never said a word against him or any of you." He fixed Maldwic with a sharp eye. "I am still a member of this company. By the rules established, I challenge you."

Maldwic's initial irritation faded when he sized up his opponent who was at least half a head shorter. "You want to challenge me?"

"Yes." Conal dismounted, handed the reins to Torgreth, and stepped into the cleared space in front of Maldwic.

"Suit yourself. Your funeral." Maldwic slid down from his saddle, handing the reins to the rider next to him.

"The challenge ends when the first person yields and the other is declared the winner," Conal said.

"I know the rules," Maldwic sneered, standing two paces away.

"I don't have a sword, so it's barehanded."

"That's fine." He unhooked his sword and handed it to the opposite rider next to him.

"You ready?"

"Anytime you are," Maldwic boasted.

Conal stuck out a hand. "Let's shake hands before we begin."

Maldwic cocked an eyebrow. "Why?"

"No hard feelings. That's all."

Immediately recognizing that he could avoid a fight simply by squeezing Conal's hand so hard that he would beg for mercy, Maldwic grasped the offered hand.

A battle of strength commenced and Maldwic was shocked by the young man's grip. The cheers for Maldwic quickly diminished as the man began sweating, pouring out all the strength he could muster, his frustration surging for Conal seemed far too relaxed.

Maldwic's knees started to tremble then buckle as his companions watched in stunned silence. Excruciating pain pulsed up his arm and his face and body tightened in anguish, yet still he gripped Conal's hand, except it was Conal who gripped *his* hand, for try as he might, he could not reciprocate the power of Conal's strength.

And then he could take no more as he felt the bones grinding against each other, the pain wracking his entire body.

Crying out, "I yield," he dropped to his knees, cradling his limp hand, gasping in heavy breaths. Tilting his head to stare up at him, his mouth gaped open. "Who are you?"

"I am Conal, the new boss of this company." He bent down to help lift him to standing. Turning to the rest of the highwaymen, he said, "Does anyone wish to challenge me?" None responded, more than a few looking at him with awe.

Swinging back up into his saddle, he waited as Maldwic struggled to pull himself up into the saddle then addressed the company. "Maldwic remains second in command. Obey him as you would me for eventually, he will become boss."

Surprised, Maldwic respectfully dipped his head.

"We ride for Denhelm. As of this moment, you are no longer Highwaymen, but respected members of an elite troop."

Thinking this a new hustle, they grinned and smirked.

Deciding it would be more trouble to tell them the truth, he returned their smiles. *Wait until they find out I'm a Cobra.*

CHAPTER 5

Gwen

Gwen was relieved when Aimil said they would wait until nightfall to escape. Her blistered feet were sore and she needed to rest. The guards opened the doors and a young elven girl entered, carrying a tray of fresh fruits, cheeses, a loaf of bread, and some wooden plates. Kirith played host and divvied up the food onto the plates, then handed them to Gwen and Aimil.

"Is this a snack?" Gwen asked.

"No. It's dinner time here, and even prisoners get fed."

"This is what elves eat for dinner? There's no meat." Gwen didn't mind fruit and cheese, but she needed something more filling to sate her hunger.

"We don't eat meat. Not unless there are no other options," Kirith said.

"What? Why not?"

"We are one with the life forces around us, and we do not believe in taking another life unnecessarily."

Gwen found that perspective entirely foreign and didn't know what to say, so she kept quiet and ate. She looked around the room while she chewed, admiring the beauty of the room. It didn't take long for her to realize that elves put intricate details into everything. Even the chairs they sat in had animals carved into the wood.

"You said this room is for visiting nobles," Gwen said. "How many elven cities are there?"

"Only a handful," Kirith answered. "Though there are many small communities across Auleavell."

Gwen plucked a few grapes from a stem and popped them into her mouth. They were perfectly ripe and flooded her mouth with sweet juices that excited her taste buds. Despite that, she was thirsty and wondered why the elven girl had neglected to bring something to drink.

"I need water," she said, looking at Kirith questioningly.

"My apologies," he replied. "I'm being a forgetful host." He rose from his chair and walked to a small table that had a silver pitcher and wooden cups. Kirith filled three of the cups and delivered two of them to Gwen and Aimil. Gwen drank deeply of the water. The cool liquid slicked her throat and she immediately felt more rejuvenated than she had in weeks. Her surprise was etched upon her face, causing Kirith to smile at her.

"The waters of the Thaestra River bring healing," he said.

"This water is magical?" Gwen asked, peering into the cup. It looked normal to her.

"Call it magic or the power of nature," Kirith said. "We care for the river, and it cares for us."

"I'd forgotten about the river," Aimil said. "I've heard that people who bathe in the water experience miracles."

"Not all who have, but there are many with such stories. We elves are used to the water, so we do not notice the difference as much. Would you like to bathe in the water? There is a tub in the corner there." Kirith nodded toward the corner of the room.

"How do you get the water up here?" Gwen asked.

"Much of the Thaestra flows underground, but magic directs it into the trees through hollowed roots. The water flows continuously, keeping the bathing tubs fresh. Try it," Kirith motioned. "It will soothe your pains."

"I don't want to get my clothes wet, especially if we're going to scale down the tree," Gwen replied. She was curious, though.

"Then remove them."

Gwen gave Kirith an odd look. He'd said that so casually as if it wouldn't be awkward for her to disrobe in front of him. He was a complete stranger.

"Elves do not view nakedness the same way we do," Aimil said, as though reading her mind. She stood and walked over to the tub, then removed her clothes and stepped into the water. Gwen averted her gaze too late and caught a glimpse of Aimil's backside, but she had practically seen the woman naked before when she had chosen her rune from Aimil's body. Still, it was embarrassing to Gwen.

"Go," Kirith encouraged. "I can sense your exhaustion. The water will help."

He seemed sincere, but Gwen wasn't sure if he was just trying to get her naked. Her feet cried out for relief, and she finally relented and went to the tub. She cast a glance at Kirith, but he wasn't looking at her. She hurriedly removed her clothes and climbed into the tub, sinking below the moving water. The temperature was neither hot nor cold, but a perfect balance between the two, and she sighed in relief.

The throbbing in her feet faded and the ache of her muscles dulled until she didn't feel weary at all.

"That's incredible," Gwen said. "I feel … perfect."

"The stories I've heard don't do it justice," Aimil said. She leaned back and stretched out with a groan.

The tub was large enough to hold at least four people comfortably. Gwen decided if all elven nobles had baths like this one, they were blessed beyond measure. She looked up at Kirith as he approached the tub. He removed his shirt and Gwen's eyes widened.

"What are you doing?" she asked, trying to keep her voice calm.

"Partaking of the waters," he said simply.

Gwen turned her gaze as Kirith removed his boots and stripped his pants off, then joined them in the tub. She swallowed hard and moved away. Elves might view nakedness differently, but Gwen didn't.

The three of them sat silently. Gwen felt awkward but Aimil and Kirith were relaxed as if they weren't all naked in front of each other.

"The message you have for Lyra … what is it about?" Kirith asked.

"I'm not sure," Gwen replied, glad to have a distraction. "My friend just asked me to deliver it to her. He said she was an ally to the rebellion."

"She is," Kirith confirmed. "Support among my people grows for her daily, but my father ignores her warnings. He would be wise to heed her words before it's too late."

Gwen found Kirith's last few words odd, but Kirith's tone hadn't implied anything ill. She looked toward the balcony and saw that the sun had almost descended. The patches of sky that were visible through the trees were vibrant orange.

"It's almost time to go," Gwen said.

"A little longer," Aimil replied. She moved closer to Kirith and ran her fingers through his hair, tucking the long strands behind his pointed ear. Kirith looked Aimil in the eyes and Gwen felt even more awkward than before. She moved past them and got out of the tub, feeling self-conscious about her body. A glance over her shoulder revealed that Kirith and Aimil weren't even paying her any attention.

Gwen looked around for something to dry off with and found a long strip of cloth hanging on the wall near the tub. She grabbed it and dried off, then put her clothes back on. They were dirty, but she didn't care. Her eyes widened when she heard the sounds of lovemaking and hurried to the balcony, trying to get as far away from the sound as possible.

She peered over the railing and eyed the descent. The ground was far below and the thought of scaling down the tree caused a flutter in Gwen's stomach. It seemed like an impossible distance. And what if she fell? Gwen chewed her bottom lip in worry. She noticed the moans from the tub had stopped, but she didn't dare turn to look.

Aimil joined her at the balcony and Gwen was relieved to see the woman was dressed.

"What was *that* about?" Gwen whispered harshly.

"I was clearing my head before we do this," Aimil replied. "And don't act like you don't have needs."

Gwen ignored the comment and continued to peer down at the ground. Darkness had settled across the landscape, obscuring the view. Gwen's heart fluttered in her chest.

"Are you sure this is a good idea?"

"Not really," Aimil replied. "But what other option do we have? Unless we can find a way to get these shackles off, I don't see how we're going to get out of here. Besides, you have to get that letter to Lyra. I don't think Falael is willingly going to let you give it to her."

The woman had valid points. Gwen breathed in deeply several times, trying to calm her pounding heart. "Let's get this over with, then."

Aimil went first, tossing one leg over the railing. She adjusted her grip and the other leg followed, then she began a slow descent along the tree. Kirith stepped onto the balcony and Gwen's cheeks flushed. He didn't seem to notice or didn't care, and he motioned after Aimil.

"Do you want to go next?"

"Yes," she replied quickly, then climbed over the railing. Gwen locked eyes with Kirith for a moment and she could feel her face burning. She tried not to think about his muscled unclothed body and failed. *Focus,* she scolded herself.

She crept down the tree much slower than Aimil. Her footing was the hardest part since she couldn't see where to place her feet and her upper body strength was almost non-existent. Gwen struggled the entire way, scaring herself a few times when she slipped. After what she felt was an eternity, her feet touched the ground.

"Took you long enough," Aimil said, though she was smiling. Kirith stood next to her and Gwen scrunched her brows, trying to figure out how he'd beaten her down without her notice.

"Where are we going?" Gwen asked, brushing her hands off on her thighs.

"Lyra's usually at the temple at sunset, so we'll look for her there first," Kirith said.

"What about guards?" Aimil looked around as if expecting a host of them to close in upon them at any moment.

"There aren't many at night. Since my father doesn't believe there are any threats to our safety, their numbers are minimal. We'll keep to the shadows regardless, just to be safe."

Kirith led them along a worn path, weaving among the trees. Gwen expected to see a few elves, but the night was quiet and no one else was out. They skirted along the edge of the forest-city, and Gwen bit back a gasp when she'd stepped too close to the border. The bracelet had grown hot against her skin, catching her by surprise.

"Watch your steps," Kirith said. "If you cross over the border, pain will be the last thing you know before you die."

Gwen was bothered by how nonchalantly he said that. How often did people get shackled? And how often did they die from trying to escape? She shuddered at the thought and intentionally kept a wider distance from the invisible border of the city.

A well-lit clearing was ahead and Kirith slowed his steps. They kept hidden in the shadows and he whistled a few notes, the sound disguised as a bird call. A moment later the same whistle echoed back.

"It's safe," Kirith said. He led them into the clearing and Gwen saw two elven guards standing at either side of the temple archway. Her heart skipped a beat and she was about to sprint in the opposite direction when they bowed low to Kirith.

"My Lord," they greeted in unison.

"Good evening," Kirith replied, offering a tilt of his head. "The city seems clear tonight."

"Quiet as a den of foxes," one of the guards said.

Kirith looked over his shoulder at Gwen and Aimil and motioned them to follow him inside. Gwen looked up at the temple, surprised that it too was built within a tree. She'd foolishly expected a building of stone with columns. The interior of the tree was bright and the walls were inscribed with designs just as detailed as the ones in the palace.

Pews lined the room on either side while a walkway stretched down the middle. The pews were formed from the tree itself and radiated magic that Gwen could feel even through her shackle. A few elves were present, their heads bowed. The place exuded peace and Gwen's worries were washed away in a wave of tranquility.

"What deity is this temple for?" Gwen whispered.

"Solara," Kirith replied. "Goddess of the Stars."

Gwen looked past him to where a large dragon statue resided. It sat upon a raised dais, a foot above the rest of the floor. Its wings were spread wide, each several feet long. The scaly body of the creature twisted back and forth from its head down to the tip of its tail. Kneeling in front of it was an elven woman. Kirith led them along the walkway and stopped a few feet behind the woman. They waited in silence until the woman finished her prayer, then she stood and turned to face them.

"Prince Kirith," she greeted warmly.

"Lyra," Kirith said. "This is Aimil and Gwen."

Lyra's slender brow rose curiously. "How did you get humans into Auleavell without your father knowing?"

"He knows," Kirith replied, pointing to the bracelets on Aimil's arm.

"Of course he does," Lyra said, a smile tugging at the corner of her lips.

Gwen studied the woman intently. There was something about her that seemed … *off,* but she didn't know what it was. She was an elf, as tall as Kirith, and just as beautiful in appearance. Her hair was golden brown and it reached down past her waist in a long elaborate braid. Her eyes were green, but they held a fierceness that Gwen found intimidating. Despite that, her voice was soft and melodic, adding to the calm atmosphere of the temple.

"Gwen has a message for you from a friend of hers," he added.

Lyra looked at Gwen expectantly. "Who sent this message?"

Gwen cleared her throat. "It's from Eradore." There was an entire speech she had prepared, but the words disappeared from her mind. She retrieved the scroll case and fumbled with it, then handed it to Lyra.

The elf opened it and unrolled the parchment, her eyes scanning over what was written. She lowered the parchment and looked at Kirith.

"If your father knows they are here, why did he let them come to me?"

"He doesn't know we're here. We snuck out of the palace."

"Clever. I assume there will be a trial?"

"Yes, tomorrow morning," Kirith replied.

"That is good. Take them back to the palace and ensure that they are present for the trial."

Gwen heard their conversation, but she wasn't listening. She was focused on Lyra. There was something … *there.* Lyra's Aspect. It wasn't green like the other elves. It was silver. She tried to get Aimil's attention, but the woman wasn't looking at her.

"Are you sure? The nobles will say they're guilty."

"I am sure," Lyra said.

Kirith was conflicted. "I promised them I would make things right. I don't want them to be executed."

"They won't be," Lyra replied.

"How do you know?"

"It's time."

"Time for what?" Kirith asked.

"It's time to implement our plan."

CHAPTER 6

Conal

Riding beside Bryok, Conal inhaled the scent of the pine forest, a fragrance that always filled him with peace. Behind him, Galadyr and Torgreth engaged in friendly antagonism as to who were better carvers, elves or dwarves. The rest of the company rode two abreast tailing behind them.

"I've been wondering," Conal said looking over at Bryok, "when we were in Morendir and you and Drustan were looking at the rune bones, you nearly fainted when you saw one set of bones in a box. Then when we packed all of them onto the wagon to take back to Monkreth, you kept that box separate, carrying it yourself. Why?"

Bryok's placid face hardened. "They were dangerous."

"Aren't all rune bones dangerous in some form or other? You said so yourself."

"These were especially dangerous, evil." His jaw clenched and his nostrils flared.

Startled at his intensity, Conal asked, "What were they?"

Bryok paused before he replied, "Dragon-lock runes."

"Dragon lock? What do they do?"

Lips pursed, Bryok inhaled an angry breath. "They bind a dragon to an individual, one consumed with evil

56

for no one of noble heart would ever bind a dragon to himself."

Conal furrowed his brow, wondering why Bryok was so angry. "It's not like they can ever be used."

"Don't be a fool," Bryok snapped.

"What's your problem?" Conal shot back. "How many dragons have you seen in your lifetime? Show me a dragon and maybe I'll worry about it. Until then, let's remain focused on the job at hand. Besides, didn't you burn those rune bones?"

"That's not the point," Bryok retorted. "Someone had those bones carved, someone with a deep knowledge of magic, someone who could ruin your chances of reclaiming a kingdom. That alone should worry you."

"Like who?"

"How should I know? But if there are Dragon-lock bones, trust me, there are worse ones already carved."

Conal suddenly realized the glaring flaw in his quest: if he could use magic, so could the enemy. Truth was, he hadn't given it much thought, assuming that Bryok or Drustan could counter anything used against them. Ever since he was imbued with his extraordinary strength and other traits, he'd begun to feel invincible. Now he wasn't so sure.

Giving voice to his thoughts, he said, "So you and Drustan are going to need help if we're to defeat Torian and his wizards."

"Drustan and I are half-druids, remember? Which means that we have only half the power of a true wizard or mage. But we are not without resources for we have friends who more than make up for our limited abilities."

Conal rode in silence for a bit, smiling at the ongoing debate behind him. Torgreth had scored an advantage when Galadyr admitted that no one carved stone like a dwarf, but quickly added that elves were without equal when it came to wood carving, causing Torgreth to begrudgingly admit that elves were mighty fine wood carvers, probably among the best.

An idea blossomed and he gazed over at Bryok. "Can I learn magic?"

Bryok shook his head. "It doesn't work that way. You either have the gift or you don't. Remember what I said back in Monkreth. Only individuals who are mage-marked can use rune bones and being mage-marked doesn't necessarily mean you are a mage."

"How do I know I am not a mage if I'm never taught how to be one?

Bryok narrowed his gaze at him. "When you look at me, what do you see?"

"Huh?"

"What do you see when you look at me?"

Puzzled, Conal studied the man riding next to him and shrugged. "I see a half-druid named Bryok with his reddish-brown hair tied behind his head." He purposely left off the 'handsome' part, not wanting to inflate the man's vanity.

"What about colors?"

"Colors?"

"Yes, do you see any color?"

"Of course I see color," Conal indignantly replied. "I can see the color of your hair, the color of your clothes, even the color of the horse you're riding. What does that have to do with anything?"

Bryok nodded with satisfaction. "You are not a mage nor a wizard and will never become one."

"How do you know?" Conal snapped, insulted by the curt dismissal.

"Do not be offended," Bryok soothed. "In fact, be thankful. Being a mage or wizard isn't without its problems. No matter how hard you try, once people find out you're a mage, people treat you differently, at arms' length, never trusting you. They call upon you when they need something then want nothing to do with you once they get what they want. You are different. You are not meant to be a mage. You are meant to rule."

Assuaged at the backhanded compliment Conal mulled the uncertain future. Casting a sly look at Bryok, he quietly said, "Have you really seen a dragon?"

"Yes," he answered, looking over his shoulder to check no one else heard the conversation. Leaning over towards him, his voice low so that only Conal could hear, he said, "There is one not too far away. If we are close enough when we stop for the night, I will take you to him."

Conal's heart skipped a beat. "Really?"

"Shhh, not so loud," Bryok grimaced. "And yes, really."

"What's he like?"

"I think it best we drop the subject for the moment," Bryok cautioned, settling back in his saddle. "There will be enough time tonight to answer your questions."

Frustrated at the reply, Conal changed topics to divert his own distraction. "Are there other runes that would be good for me to have?"

"Most runes deal in the physical realm, like increasing strength and stamina, or special weapon abilities. Thus, if you want to add to the abilities you now have, you need to think in terms of the physical. What other physical skills would you want?"

Conal pondered only a moment. "I was thinking along the lines of what would a Cobra need? Things like stealth, maybe a knowledge of poisons, stuff like that."

"Stealth is possible," Bryok replied, "but knowledge of poisons is something you'll have to learn yourself. Remember the restrictions concerning the physical."

"But you said *most*," Conal countered.

"I know where you're going with this," Bryok objected, holding a hand up. "Making the leap to the spirit world requires the person be some type of magician, like a mage or a wizard. That's why the Dragon-lock rune bones are so dangerous."

"Because only a mage can use them?"

"Only a very powerful mage," Bryok corrected.

Conal frowned. "So why were they in Morendir? All Havyrd had was his voice. Once that was taken away, he was nothing."

"I know," Bryok said, slowly nodding. "That's what concerns me. Why would someone put such powerful rune-bones there?"

"Maybe they thought it was a safe place, away from prying eyes," Conal offered.

"Hey you two," Torgreth called out. "We need an unbiased judge. Who's the better carvers, elves or dwarves?"

"They're both good," Conal replied without thinking.

Torgreth snorted a laugh and leaned towards Galadyr. "That's what my Mum used to say when me and Voldar brought carvings to her to tell us which one was the best. Never did choose a winner. Stopped asking her after a while."

"That's because you both carve in different media," Conal explained. "To make value judgment, we'd need to see a stone carving by an elf and a wood carving by a dwarf. Then we could judge fairly."

"That was profound," Torgreth teased. "I'm impressed."

Ignoring him, Conal asked Bryok, "Where should we spend the night?"

"About halfway to Denhelm, near the ruins of Glaston," Bryok replied, understanding the reason for the question. "At this pace we should get there after dark."

"We need to pick up the pace then," Conal suggested.

"Your call," Bryok replied.

Increasing the pace to a trot and taking occasional rests, they arrived at the outskirts of the ruins in the late afternoon. Conal was more than ready to get off the saddle.

"We camp here tonight," he announced.

"Here?" several voices nervously complained.

"Here," Maldwic asserted. "Where do you want us to set up, Boss?"

"You decide, Maldwic," Conal answered, sitting on his horse, surveying the ruins of what had once been a thriving city.

Centuries of war had ravaged the city. Lichen and ivy covered the walls, broken in places, a testament to the battering rams and trebuchet stone missiles. The gates, ripped from their hinges, lay inside the barbican. Weeds and trees had reclaimed much of the city streets and parks. The present residents consisted of rodents, coyotes, and the occasional bear. When the last assault had slaughtered the remaining living defenders and citizens, the city was pronounced accursed. Stories grew of the dead roaming the homes and castle, unsettled and unable to find rest.

Though dismissing the stories as fabled imagination, the place still gave Conal the creeps.

"It's still a little bit of a ride," Bryok quietly relayed.

"Maldwic," Conal called out to his subordinate.

"Yes, Boss?" Maldwic guided his horse to come alongside him.

"Bryok and I have some business to attend to. We'll be back after it's dark. Don't worry," he added, seeing the doubt on the man's face, "Bryok's a druid. We'll be safe."

"OK, Boss."

"Where're we setting up?"

"In the barbican. It's big enough for all of us and gives us better protection."

"Fine. See you in a bit."

"Take this." Maldwic handed him a short sword encased in a leather scabbard. "I had it as an extra. Figured you might need it."

"Thank you, Maldwic." He buckled the sword around his waist. "Give the company a name. Something strong and noble. Something like 'Maldwic's Marauders.' That has a punch to it."

"But you're the boss," he countered, though flattered with the suggested name.

"Only for a little while. Besides, I have bigger plans in mind. I'll be back shortly."

While Maldwic reined his horse around to give instructions to the company, Torgreth piped up, "Where you going?"

"We have some things to discuss," Bryok answered, giving Galadyr a knowing look, receiving a nod of understanding in return.

"You can't discuss them here?" Torgreth cocked an eyebrow.

Galadyr placed a gentle hand on the dwarf's shoulder. "It is something that needs to be discussed far enough away from prying ears."

Torgreth twisted his head up to give him a curious stare. "How do you know?"

"I don't," he blandly replied, "but I trust them enough not to interfere."

Torgreth blinked at the revelation and grinned. "Point noted. Guess I'd better find a place to settle before all these thieves get the good spots. Come along elf. I've got extra leaf if you got a pipe."

Conal followed Bryok as the druid rode the edges of the city walls to the north-east where the heavily forested mountains rose and then onto a little used path that snaked its way through the evergreens and hardwoods, repeatedly curling back on itself as it ascended.

"Can you tell me anything about the dragon?" Conal finally asked, his curiosity bursting.

"His name is Krag," Bryok answered, "Krag the Patient One or sometimes Krag the Wise, though now, he is merely Krag. He is a Forest Dragon."

"Forest Dragon? How many kinds are there?"

"At one time there were many," Bryok explained, a great melancholy in his voice, "all different sizes. Some were small, the size of the largest draft horse. Others were large, like the Mountain Dragons, and some even larger, like Rock Dragons."

"So how big is a forest dragon."

"You will see when you meet him."

"What's he like?"

Bryok frowned in thought. "He can be gruff at times, but you have to understand all that he has seen, all that he has endured."

"Do you think he will help us?"

"That will be up to you to convince him."

"Me?" Conal blurted. "Why me?

"Because you are the king's son. While I think about it, I would not mention that you bear the Cobra brand... at least not yet."

"Why not?

"Remember the prophecy?"

"The eagle will bear the vipers in its claws, yet from the west a cobra will rise and strike down the eagle," Conal intoned. "Yes, I remember. So what?"

"So, let's just keep quiet about that for now, shall we?" Bryok sternly replied.

"Why?"

Bryok heaved a long-suffering sigh. "Because the Cobra part implies that the vipers, or the king's children will be dominated by the Cobra."

"No it doesn't," Conal argued. "All it says is that the Cobra will strike down the eagle. It says nothing about ruling or anything else."

Bryok flipped an inpatient hand at him. "You just don't understand."

"What's to understand? And how do you even know this prophecy is about me and Torian?" Conal said with a dismissive shake of his head.

"Can we drop it for now?" Bryok snapped. "Just don't mention it, OK?"

"OK, OK, mum's the word."

Silence ruled for a few minutes before Conal asked, "What else can you tell me about him?"

"Be respectful when you talk to him. Though you are a king's son, he too is royalty, a prince at one time. And remember, we need his help."

"Why? How can he help if he's spending his life hiding?"

Bryok shot him a look of irritation. "He is waiting, like the few remaining survivors, for a true king to rise up, one that will establish peace, a peace where dragons are free to live without fear of being hunted."

Conal pondered the answer. "Seems to me you're putting a lot of faith into a tiny fraction of our effort. Dragons have been hiding because they've been hunted almost to extinction. And now you think they're going to want to help us?"

Bryok jerked his horse to a halt. "Do you want to see this dragon or not? I have half a mind to turn around and not waste my time." He thrust a finger at Conal. "Dragons were hunted to near extinction because no one saw any need for them. It's hard to stay alive when everyone is out to kill you. Would you feel the same way if humans were the target of extermination?"

Conal held up his hands in defeat. "OK, you win."

Prodding his horse forward, Bryok huffed, "Use your brains. Dragons have great powers. How can we best use them to achieve what we need?"

Fading sunlight rimed the mountain tops as Bryok led them into a wide clearing. Conal glanced around at the pleasant meadow. Wildflowers undulated in the gentle wind. The cloudless sky above added to the aura of peace. Securing their mounts back down the path, Bryok led Conal to the middle of the field.

"You wait here while I go see if Krag is willing to show himself."

"Why can't I come a long?"

Bryok heaved a sigh of exasperation. "Have you not been listening? They don't trust anyone. Just stay here."

"OK."

Conal watched Bryok stalk across the field then disappear into the woods. For some reason, Conal expected an immediate appearance, as though the dragon was hiding in the forest at the edge of the meadow. When minutes passed and the daylight began to fade, Conal grew concerned. What if something had happened to Bryok? Suppose they were in the wrong place? What if the dragon was hiding somewhere else and was no longer there?

Knowing it was futile to go look for him, he debated calling out when a gigantic, winged creature filled the darkening sky above him, circling slowly before plummeting to the ground to stand towering over Conal, causing him to stumble backwards.

"So, you're the one," Krag said, his voice rich and resonant. He sat back on his haunches and folded his wings behind him, his tail curling around him. "Tell me human, why should I trust you?"

CHAPTER 7

Gwen

Gwen spent most of the night tossing and turning, her anxious thoughts making her mind run wild. It didn't help that Kirith hadn't answered her questions about the plan that Lyra mentioned.

Lyra.

Gwen knew there was something more to the woman. Her Aspect alone was an oddity, but it was more than that. She wished she could figure it out, but whatever *it* was, it continued to elude her. Aimil hadn't seemed to notice anything out of the ordinary, but Aimil had traveled to many places. Gwen considered the possibility that she was overthinking things.

When dawn came, she hadn't slept much. She was surprised to find that all of her aches and pains were gone, a blessing from bathing in the Thaestra water. The same young elven woman from the previous day made another appearance, bringing a tray full of food for breakfast. The options were the same, mostly fruits, and Gwen forced herself to accept that she would have to wait for meat until they returned to human lands.

If they returned at all.

"The nobles are arriving for the trial," Kirith said from the balcony. "It won't be long now."

Gwen thought back to when they found him with the vagabonds. His hair was been matted with dried blood and he'd looked ragged. Even so, Gwen had still seen his beauty, had felt his regality shine through the roughness. Now that he was cleaned up, it shined doubly so. His hair had a natural glow to it and his eyes held an excitement she didn't understand. And he and Aimil shared something now, didn't they?

"Are you still refusing to tell us what this plan entails?" Gwen asked, trying to stay focused.

"Trust me," Kirith said, stepping back into the main room. "I would never allow you to enter the path of danger in my homeland."

Trust him. Those words reminded Gwen of Tobias and a twinge of pain pulled at her heart. She closed her eyes for a moment and gritted her teeth against the hurt, waiting for it to pass, then opened her eyes again.

"I'm sorry if I have angered you." Kirith was staring at her.

"It's not that," Gwen replied. "Or you. It's nothing."

Kirith bowed his head but Gwen could tell he was curious about her reaction. She picked up an apple from the tray and bit into it. The crisp skin broke under her teeth, showering her tongue with a rush of sweet juice. She devoured the rest of the apple and waited.

The young elven woman returned, this time bearing a purple robe. Kirith let her put it on him, then said something in another language to her. Gwen assumed it was elvish. It sounded musical and tickled her ears. The young elf bowed to him, a smile playing at her lips, then left.

"Who is that?" Aimil asked.

"That is my sister, Talahna."

"She's a servant?" Gwen asked.

Kirith laughed loudly. "Talahna is not a servant," he replied. "She's—"

His words were cut off as the doors opened fully and a host of guards, including Haladavar, strode inside.

"My Lord," Haladavar greeted Kirith. "The court awaits your presence."

"Lead the way," Kirith replied.

The guards were wearing extravagant capes and their chainmail armor gleamed as if it had been polished. Their demeanor was solemn, their expressions serious. Gwen felt as though the trial was some sort of sacred ceremony judging by the change of atmosphere. Kirith stepped into the hall, followed by Aimil, then Gwen. Haladavar took the lead and the host of guards moved into position around the three prisoners.

Gwen didn't recognize anything they passed, but their arrival and detainment had been such a blur. She admired everything about Auleavell. Everything except King Falael. Kirith was so different from his father that she was tempted to question whether Kirith was truly from Falael's loins. The fact that they were so similar in appearance was the only reason she didn't.

They walked down the stairs, all the way to the bottom floor. It was crowded with elves, both nobles and commoners, and guards lined the walls around the entire room. Falael was at the center of the room seated on a chair made of tree roots. It curved gracefully up from the floor and Gwen marveled at it, but she didn't think the chair looked very comfortable. It appeared to be more for looks than functionality.

The crowd was gathered around the center, but a ring of guards around Falael kept everyone from getting too close to him. Apparently, Falael didn't trust his own people. Haladavar escorted them through the crowd and stopped outside the ring of guards. Falael stood up and the room went silent.

"Welcome, nobles of Auleavell. Today we must decide the fate of two criminals, but we must also choose a punishment for our wayward prince."

The ring of guards parted and Haladavar led Kirith to Falael's side. Gwen scanned the crowd, looking at the faces of the nobles. They looked proud and haughty just like their king. She looked at Aimil and had to hide her smile. The woman wore an expression that dared someone to test her anger.

"What are the charges against them?" one of the nobles asked.

"Trespassing," Falael answered. "And as everyone here knows, that means they must be executed."

There was a general murmur of agreement throughout the room. Gwen turned her gaze to Falael, her anger rising at his words.

"They weren't trespassing," Kirith said loudly. The room went silent again, but this time Gwen noticed it was from shock. "They rescued me from bandits who thought to collect a bounty on my head. A bounty put out by my father, no less."

"He speaks out of turn despite knowing the law," Falael said. "Lyra's poisoning of his mind, and the minds of our children, must end. She has already been banned from this court, but clearly, that is not enough. We must force her from Auleavell."

"Excommunication!" someone shouted.

71

The word was repeated by others until the room echoed with it. Falael raised his hand, calling for order.

"I agree," Falael said. "Every noble who votes in favor, raise your right hand."

Gwen was surprised to see how many arms went up across the room. Lyra was odd, sure, but that didn't mean she should be removed from her own home.

"It is decided. Lyra Talinos has been excommunicated." Falael looked at Haladavar. "Find her and remove her."

The tone in his voice sent a shiver down Gwen's back. His command sounded more like an order for death. Haladavar bowed low and motioned to a few guards, who followed him out of the chamber. Gwen wasn't sure how any of this fit into some sort of plan.

"Now, back to the humans," Falael said. "They were caught trespassing with Prince Kirith as their prisoner. Haladavar himself found them and brought them here for trial. Every noble who votes them as guilty, raise your right hand."

Gwen's heart sank into her stomach as every noble in the room raised their hand into the air. Aimil turned to the elves closest to her and shot them stares of death. A few of them stepped further away, but others ignored her.

"We need to escape," Gwen said to Aimil. "Whatever Lyra and Kirith had planned isn't happening now."

"Where do you plan to go?" Aimil asked. "We're bound here as long as we have these bracelets on, remember?"

Gwen had forgotten. She tugged on her bracelet futilely while she looked around the room, trying to plot out the best route of escape. There were too many guards and too many obstacles between them and the exit.

"It is also decided," Falael's voice echoed throughout the room. "The humans are guilty and will be executed by nightfall." There was a low rumble of approval from the nobles. "Lastly, we must decide upon a just punishment for our prince. He has allowed the lies from Lyra's mouth to pollute his mind and has even spoken evil in my presence. Who here would like to suggest his chastisement?"

Several nobles raised their hands and spoke at the same time. Falael smiled and it made Gwen's stomach churn. He was enjoying the spectacle. The fact that he found delight at the prospect of his own son's torment was something Gwen couldn't fathom.

"There will be no such punishment issued," an angry voice said. Gwen turned to see who had spoken and gasped when she saw Lyra striding through the archway. The crowd of elves parted to let her pass, but some of the guards along the wall rushed to stop her.

"Halt!" she demanded. The guards hesitated and even Gwen felt the authority in her voice. She wanted to obey Lyra and she wasn't even moving.

"Stop her!" Falael said. "Remove her from this chamber!"

"Guards!" It was Kirith shouting. "Nobles! It is time to rise!"

The room erupted in chaos. Guards turned on one another, as well as the nobles, snapping the magic negating bracelets onto their wrists. Gwen drew close to Aimil for safety, but the elves were too preoccupied with their fellows to care about them. Kirith rushed his father and put a bracelet onto Falael's wrist as the clang of steel rang out. The factions of guards struggled, those loyal to father and son pitted against one another.

"It's a coupe," Aimil said, a hint of surprise in her voice. "Kirith is taking the throne."

Gwen wondered if they were the cause of it all, but then she remembered Lyra's plan. This must have been what she meant. She looked for the woman in the crowd and saw her heading for Falael.

"I think it's about to get bloody in here," Gwen said. "We should get out into the open."

"No," Aimil replied. "I want to see what happens."

Before Gwen could make up her mind about fleeing the tree, Lyra grabbed Kirith's hand and lifted it.

"Hail your new king, Auleavell!"

A cheer ran out and Gwen realized the battle was over just as quickly as it began. Kirith's supporters had subdued the others.

"I excommunicate you!" Falael snarled at Kirith. "You are banished from this court!"

"No, father," Kirith replied calmly. "It is *you* who is banished from this court. The people have spoken this day. You and those loyal to you are hereby stripped of your titles and powers. As king of Auleavell, I rescind the excommunication of Lyra and grant Gwen and Aimil their freedom. They are friends of Auleavell and are welcome in our lands at any time, with or without invitation."

"You can't do this," Falael said. "You have no authority!"

"Your age must be getting to your mind," Kirith replied. "I just did it." He motioned to one of his guards. "Take him away."

Falael was led up the stairs first, then the other nobles were escorted from the room. Those nobles loyal to Kirith remained and he bestowed the titles and lands of those arrested to them.

"May it be remembered that the king of Auleavell is the voice of the people. When that voice fails in its duty, another will speak in its place. Let everyone here never forget this lesson."

As the crowd began to disperse, Kirith joined Gwen and Aimil. Two guards stayed at his side.

"Thank you for trusting me," he said. "Lyra and I laid this plan out before I was captured. I knew my father would never realize that Torian is a threat, so I did what I had to for my people and yours."

"I am sure Eradore and the rest of the rebellion will be proud to call you an ally," Gwen said. "I'm sorry that you had to usurp your father."

"It is my hope that my father will come to see reason while he is locked up. If he can, then I may be tempted to step down and let him rule again."

"Though I do not believe he will, it is a heartfelt sentiment," Lyra said as she approached them.

Gwen looked at her and saw the silver glow of her Aspect. She wanted to ask her about it, but it didn't feel like the right time. Instead, she offered Lyra a smile and then turned her attention back to Kirith.

"Can we have these removed?" Gwen asked, lifting her arm and nodding at the bracelet.

"Of course," Kirith replied.

One of his guards removed the bracelet from Gwen and the other freed Aimil. Gwen felt the magic surge back into her mind, its steady pulse thrumming in the rune on her hand. It reminded her that she might find another rune before she left for Steepcross.

"Are there any mages here?" Gwen asked.

"There are a few," Kirith said. "Would you like to meet with one?"

"Yes. I was hoping to gain another rune if anyone is willing."

"You and Aimil are my honored guests. Nothing will be kept from you."

"Nothing?" Aimil asked. Her tone reminded Gwen of the previous night when she and Kirith had … Gwen's cheeks flushed in embarrassment at the memory.

"Nothing," Kirith confirmed.

"I would like to see the Thaestra River."

Kirith's eyes widened briefly. "It is forbidden to outsiders … but I will make an exception for you. I must attend to a few things, but I will meet you back here in an hour. Do you plan to come as well?" Kirith asked, looking at Gwen.

"I would love to after meeting with one of your mages. Is that all right?"

"That is agreeable. Lyra, would you mind showing Gwen to the mage you think best suited for her?"

"I know just the one," Lyra replied. "And since it is still early, I know exactly where to find him."

"Thank you," Gwen said to Kirith.

"It is I who should thank you. The both of you. If you hadn't rescued me, I think we'd find ourselves in a completely different place right now." Kirith looked at Aimil. "Feel free to wander until I return."

"I'll occupy myself," Aimil smiled.

"Follow me," Lyra said, heading for the archway that led out of the tree. Gwen hurried after her, staring uncertainly at her Aspect. She had noticed that Lyra was the only elf she'd seen with one that wasn't green. They left the tree and followed a path that forked to the left. Lyra slowed her pace so that Gwen could match her strides.

"I'm not blind to your mistrust," Lyra said.

"I didn't say I don't trust you," Gwen replied.

"You don't have to. I know why you stare at me so."

"Why is that?"

Lyra lowered her voice. "Because you see that I am not an elf."

CHAPTER 8

Conal

Conal craned his head back to stared into a pair of coal bright eyes high above him. "Uh... where's Bryok?" he managed to say.

"He keeps watch over my hiding spot while I am here," Krag replied. "A wise precaution, don't you think?"

"Certainly," Conal answered, still in awe as he took in the size of the beast, "especially from the way things have been going around here lately."

"Lately?" Krag snorted a dismissive laugh.

"Well... maybe longer than that," Conal sheepishly admitted before blurting, "what kind of dragon are you?"

The question surprised, yet pleased Krag. "I am a forest dragon."

"Wish it was daylight so I could see you better."

"I can see you just fine," Krag replied with a hint of humor.

"That's because you can see in the dark."

Again, Krag was surprised. "How is it that you know this?"

"I used to read about dragons when I was young," Conal answered.

"Young?" Krag laughed. "In dragon years, you are still a baby."

"I know," Conal chuckled.

"Tell me then, if you have read so much about dragons, why did you believe they did not exist?"

"How did... ah, Bryok told you that." Conal stepped closer. "I suppose I was swayed by the absence of dragons for so many years. As is our habit, when something is missing for so long, we believe it no longer exists. Then the so-called experts begin writing about dragons of the past and it doesn't take much effort to believe there are no dragons anymore."

Krag bent his head down to within inches of Conal's face, his large glowing eyes staring directly at him. "I sense something different about you. Place you hand on my forehead."

Conal reached a hand up, feeling the smoothness of the hardened scales and bumps on the dragon's forehead then flattened his hand.

Krag closed his eyes and darkness swallowed the meadow.

"I feel an imbalance in you," Krag said, "something about who you are." He opened his eyes. "You are unsure of who you are. Deep inside you, you know, but you are unconvinced. It's like you are waiting for something to happen that will settle it once and for all."

Conal jerked his hand back. "How can you tell that? I didn't feel anything."

"You were expecting our connection to hurt, like some rune bone?" He sniffed a laugh. "I am a dragon, not some incantation scratched into a dried brittle bone.

If I wanted, I could have bound you to me for the rest of your life."

Startled, Conal stepped back.

"It's not what you think,' Krag reassured him.

"You don't know what I think," Conal retorted.

"First," Krag asserted, his voice firm, "bonding with a dragon is a rare privilege that very few experience. Second, humans being violent creatures by nature, what makes you think I would want to bond with you? Third –"

"I get it," Conal snapped. "You're a powerful dragon who could impose his will on me. In fact, you're so powerful you've been hiding like a scared rabbit for the past 150 years." It came out before he could stop himself. Already he was imagining Bryok cringing at his stupidity.

"Scared rabbit," Krag thundered, rising up on his rear legs, his wings unfurling.

Refusing to be intimidated, Conal folded his arms across his chest. "Yeah, a scared rabbit. I'm still trying to figure out why Bryok was so keen on enlisting your help. If you're so powerful, why are you hiding? Why not just come out and assert yourself? Demand to be accepted."

Wisps of smoke puffed out from Krag's nostrils. "Easy for you to say, human."

"I have a name," Conal tartly reminded him.

Krag eyes flamed then settled as he sat back down and folded his wings. "Tell me, Conal, what would you do when everyone went out of their way to try and kill you? Suppose elves and dwarves suddenly made a pact to destroy humans and you found yourself one of the last humans left. Would you be so bold as to stand out in public and 'demand to be accepted'?"

"But I'm not as powerful as you are," Conal countered.

"When the forces of evil are marshaled against you, it doesn't matter how strong you are. When the odds are tens of thousands to one, what are your chances of winning? We few who remain know that our time is running out. In time, dragons *will* be a thing of the past. I and a few others have gone into hiding because there is no one who will join us, no one who will stand firm and say, 'No more.'"

"I will."

Krag gazed kindly at the young man. "You? Who are you that I should place my hope?"

"I am a king's son, *the* king's son," Conal stoutly affirmed.

Krag paused and smiled. "So, you now accept who you are?"

"Not you too," Conal groaned.

"Someone else remind you to accept who you are?"

"Bryok. The man's infuriating because he's always right. Don't tell him I said that."

Krag chuckled. "So, Conal, king's son, what is your quest?"

"Odd as it sounds, I'm going to reclaim my throne."

"Which one is that?"

"The one Torian now usurps."

"Torian?" Krag jerked upright. "You are Kamron's son?"

"So they say."

"Are you or not?" The bright eyes flickered.

Conal hesitated. He had said it once already. Why was it so hard to say again? He was being noble when he told Krag that he would stand with him. If he said it now, it meant that he had to accept it, believe it, embrace it.

Inhaling a slow breath, he answered, "I am he."

Krag rose to his back legs and flapped his wings. "It's about time."

"About time for what?" Conal asked, raising an eyebrow.

Krag settled and stretched out before him, his huge face several feet away. "What you seek to do is fraught with danger. Do you know the prophecy?"

"Yes." Conal remembered Bryok's warning to say nothing about his Cobra brand.

"Then you know you will fall into Torian's hands. Your fate will depend on the one who is the Cobra."

"Wouldn't that be *our* fate?"

Krag nodded. "A wise answer." He abruptly jerked his head back, twitching side to side, sniffing the air. "Someone's coming. They're close." He thrust himself into the air, calling out, "Bryok knows where to find me."

As Krag rose into the air, shouts bellowed from the opposite side of the clearing.

"There he is. Shoot him, quick! Aim fer the heart."

Arrows shot skyward as half a dozen men burst onto the meadow, firing madly at the dragon swirling and rising above them. Some arrows bounced harmlessly off Krag's thick skin, others arced and fell back to the earth.

Enraged, Conal raced across the field, unsheathing his sword as he ran. Too late, the attackers shifted their efforts as the dervish burst upon them. The speed and precision of his attack as he cut and slashed sent five men to their quick deaths.

Seeing his comrades cut down one and two at a time, the last man took to his heels, jettisoning his bow and quiver and racing back into the woods.

Conal stood in the middle of the carnage, his chest heaving as his anger dissipating. Looking up into the sky, he prayed Krag was unharmed and secure in his hiding place. A rising three-quarter moon gave light to the meadow. Glancing back down, he counted the bodies of the men he had just killed. Five. Five bodies lay mangled at his feet. It was then he noticed long hair on the body closest to him. Using his foot, he flipped the still warm corpse over revealing the tortured face of a young woman.

His first reaction was overwhelming guilt. Not only had he killed again, he had killed a woman.

"Conal?" Bryok called out, pushing a man ahead of him into the clearing. "You OK?"

"I'm fine," he responded, forcibly pushing his remorse aside.

"I intercepted this one on the way back here," Bryok explained, frog-marching the man to where Conal stood.

Once again Conal was surprised for the man turned out to be a woman, a little shorter than he, lithe with sharp features. Yet there was something odd about her. Though she had the look of a cornered hare, there was a fascination with Bryok, bordering on slavish wonder.

Bryok looked down at the bodies. "Watch her," he commanded as he knelt down to examine a body, picking up a limp hand to scrutinize it. He repeated the process with the others before standing to confront the woman. "Show me your hand."

When the woman didn't respond but grinned stupidly at him, he grabbed her hand, causing her to yelp. He thrust the hand towards her face and twisted it around so she could see the back of her hand. "What is this?"

The loopy smile still plastered on her face, the woman stared at her hand then at him. She reached a hand out to touch his face.

Batting the hand away, he twisted the other around for Conal to see and jabbed a finger at the tattoo of a dragon's head with a lance through it. "She's a dragon hunter."

"At one time I might have thought that an absurd occupation," Conal said, 'but not anymore. Seems sort of strange that after all these years of no one ever seeing a dragon they suddenly show up here at this very moment." He frowned at the woman. "What's wrong with her?"

Bryok twisted her arm to show the runes on the inside of her forearm. "She's been rune-marked." He heaved a sigh of disgust. "Haven't seen these in a long time. It marks the person as a dragon hunter, but the person is spirit bound to the owner of the rune bone. Back when dragon hunting was all the rage, there were lots of these kinds of people, all chasing the elusive dragon, reaping large rewards, only to discover too late that their lives were inextricably linked to their rune master. They spent their days searching for something they could never find, eventually dying out until there were no more dragon hunters. In the end, all the riches they thought they had belonged to the rune master, for they were compelled to search, never finding rest."

"So why now?" Conal asked. "Why the sudden appearance of dragon hunters?"

Bryok glanced back towards the mountain where Krag lived in hiding. "I think someone has discovered that dragons still exist and that they're on your side."

"Torian?"

"Seems logical."

Conal gazed at the woman. "What do we do with her?"

Bryok gripped the woman's wrist in his hand. In a speed almost too fast for Conal to see, Bryok jerked the woman's arm causing her to lurch forward. At the same time, he delivered a chop to her throat before spinning around with a slicing knife-hand to her neck with such a force that it broke her neck.

"My God," Conal startled as the woman wobbled as if suspended in midair before crumpling to a heap. "You killed her. Why'd you kill her?"

"She's a dragon hunter," Bryok coldly answered.

"Yes, but –"

"But what? She came here to kill Krag. She failed because you were here. You killed the others and now you're shocked because I killed her?"

"But she didn't have a chance to defend herself," Conal objected.

"She ran as soon as she saw which way the battle went," Bryok reminded him. "Had she lived, she would have told Torian about Krag and about us, about where we were and then returned to the hunt again. She was rune-bound. She had no other choice. What you should be worried about is how many other dragon hunters are out there?"

Conal knew he was right. The woman was a threat. One thing puzzled him. "Why are you so keen on enlisting dragon help? Seems to me that they're going to be more of a problem because we have to protect them."

"Did you learn nothing in your talk with Krag?" Bryok sourly asked.

"Actually, no," Conal replied. "We barely got talking when they arrived. Speaking of 'they,' what do we do with them?"

"Leave them. It's obvious they were not killed by a dragon. Anyone coming up here will be on guard and want to move on through as quickly as possible. We should go back." He led the way across the field and down the path to their horses who were calmly waiting for them.

"Surprised they didn't take fright," Conal commented.

"They know when there's danger," Bryok answered, "and when they're safe."

"One thing still puzzles me," Conal said, swinging up into the saddle. "How did they know Krag was here? If a dragon is so good at hiding that everyone thinks they no longer exist, how is it that they knew to look here?"

"That too concerns me," Bryok grimly nodded.

They rode back in silence, each lost in his own thoughts. As they approached the ruins, Conal sniffed the air. "I smell campfire smoke. Not very smart for security."

"Hey Boss," a female voice called out as the woman stepped from behind the gate pillar before the barbican.

"Hullo, Seren" Conal quietly replied, dismounting then leading his horse to the gate.

"Horses are over there." She pointed to the opposite end of the barbican. "Everyone's sleep 'cept for me and another roving guard."

"Why is there a fire?" Conal pointed at the circle of stones surrounding the rippling embers of a fire.

"Maldwic thought you might need some help returning in the dark."

"That was a good idea," Bryok interrupted.

Deciding he was tired and ready to find a spot to stretch out, Conal started to lead his horse to the tether line when the woman spoke.

"Had some folks come by not long after you left," she said. "Four men and two women."

Conal jerked to a halt. "Who were they?"

Seren started snickering. "Called themselves dragon hunters. Can you believe it? Who'd they think would fall for that? And they were serious as can be. Got mad when we laughed at 'em. And when they said there were dragons close by, we knew they were loony."

"Where are they?"

"Oh," she chuckled, "we sent them off. Maldwic sent an escort with them to make sure they got as far away from here as possible. Haven't seen 'em since. And that was just after you left. You didn't see 'em did you?"

"No," Conal answered, a little quicker than needed.

"One odd thing though," she commented. "They said they were looking for you."

"For me?" Conal sputtered.

"No, not you Boss, him." She pointed a finger and narrowed her gaze at Bryok. "They were looking for you."

CHAPTER 9

Gwen

"You're not an elf?" Gwen asked. She stopped walking and stared at Lyra suspiciously. "What do you mean?"

"Keep quiet," Lyra snapped, glancing around to see if anyone had taken an interest in their conversation. The few elves nearby were going about their business and Lyra turned her eyes back on Gwen. "It's not important."

"I think it is," Gwen replied. "Especially if you want me to trust you."

"There are many things in this life that you will never be privy to. If I trust *you,* then I will reveal what I mean. In time. Now come along."

Gwen felt the power of Lyra's authority like she had in the trial and followed her. She'd never been one to argue, and this day proved no different. They wound along the worn path that twisted through the forest-city, past the temple they had met at the night before, and stopped at the natural entrance to what Gwen assumed was a garden.

"Virion tends this place," Lyra said. "He is a wise mage and many elves come from afar to seek his advice."

"Will he grant me a rune?" Gwen asked.

"That is yet to be seen. If he thinks you are fit for one, he will grant it."

"Kirith said we would not be denied anything. Does he not rule over Virion?"

"You like to play with childish talk," Lyra said. "Do you not feel as dumb as you sound? Surely you hear your own words."

Gwen's face flushed with embarrassment and anger, but before she could recover her wits and offer a retort, a handsome elf came into view. She bit her tongue and watched him in silence. He knelt in front of a wooden lattice and lifted a wilting vine in his hand. A moment later, the vine was fully restored.

"How did he do that?" Gwen asked, her anger washed away under a wave of amazement and curiosity.

"Ask him," Lyra said.

Gwen stepped uncertainly through the entrance of the garden and approached Virion, stopping a few paces away. She waited for him to acknowledge her, but he quietly continued his healing work with the grapevines. Gwen could hear him humming lowly. At first, she thought it was an insect, but as he walked around to the other side of the lattice, she heard the sound clearly. Gwen watched him work and tried to remain patient, and even glanced questioningly over her shoulder at Lyra. The woman offered nothing in her expression.

"What is your name?" Virion suddenly asked.

Gwen snapped her head back around to look at him. His hands were still tending to the vine, but his head was turned in her direction. The first thing she noticed about him was his eyes. They were gray, close in color to his long hair, except his hair shimmered with life.

"You're blind?" Gwen blurted out. She immediately felt stupid for saying it.

Virion chuckled, not taking offense. "Yes, I am blind."

"I'm sorry. It … surprised me. My name is Gwen." She wished Lyra would have mentioned something before she made a fool of herself.

"There is nothing to apologize for. Tell me, Gwen. What brings you here?"

"I'm seeking a rune," she replied.

"Ah, a fellow mage. Welcome to my humble garden," Virion offered a slight bow. "What kind of rune are seeking?"

Gwen paused. She hadn't given it much thought. She'd gained lightning from Aimil, but that wasn't necessarily her choice. She'd merely picked a rune from among hundreds on a whim, not knowing what it did.

"I'm not sure," she confessed.

"That's not necessarily a bad thing," Virion replied. "Perhaps I can help you decide. Come closer."

Gwen did as he asked and Virion reached out a hand.

"Let me feel your runes."

"I only have one," Gwen said as she placed her hand in his. He ran his fingers over the outline of her rune and Gwen could feel power radiating from Virion. The elf was blind, but Gwen knew he wasn't helpless.

"Lightning," Virion said. "Your single rune is a weapon?"

Gwen couldn't tell by his tone whether he was impressed or bothered by that. "I didn't choose it," she replied. "Well, I did choose that rune, but I didn't know beforehand what it was."

"You chose at random?"

"Not really. I was asked to look over many runes and pick the one that stood out most. It turned out to be lightning."

"That's a fascinating way of choosing a rune," Virion said. "Are you disappointed with what you received?"

"No. It has helped me."

"How has a weapon of war helped you?"

"It helped me during a battle," Gwen answered vaguely.

"The rune fulfilled its purpose, as does all magic. Thank you for entertaining my questions, Gwen. Runes are powerful and should not be entrusted lightly. If you had to choose between a weapon of war and a tool for nature, which would you choose?"

Gwen considered the question carefully. Given what the future held with the plans of the rebellion, it would make sense that she should choose another rune that could cause destruction. Yet, if this was a test, Virion may refuse to give her a rune at all depending on her answer. She wanted more runes to aid in the struggle against Torian, and she didn't want to lie to Virion. If he chose not to give her a rune, so be it.

"I would choose a weapon of war," Gwen said.

Virion released her hand. "I am not surprised by your answer. I can sense turmoil around you. Is it fear that drives you to the arms of destruction, or something else?"

"I don't think I am headed to the arms of destruction," Gwen said, but as she spoke the words, she doubted the truth behind them. It was entirely possible that she was on the road to devastation by trying to take down a king. She'd already lost so much and she felt as though her journey had just begun.

"Who can know whether that is true or not? I will grant you a rune, Gwen, but it will not be a weapon of war."

"Thank you," Gwen said. She was a little disappointed, but he had agreed to give her a rune.

"The rune I grant you is a tool that will help the world around you. Humans cause chaos wherever they go, but it is my hope that this rune will help balance you. You have seen Auleavell. What do you think of it?"

"It's beautiful," Gwen answered.

"I am glad you think so. To balance the chaos of lightning, I give you a rune of earthen power. Close your eyes."

Gwen did so. She flinched slightly when Virion's fingers touched her temples. A flood of green glowing energy filled her mind. It reminded her of the Aspect of the elves.

"You feel the rune," he said.

"Yes," Gwen replied. It swirled around her, whispering. She couldn't understand the words, but they gave her a feeling of renewal and growth.

"Speak its name."

"*Saol,*" Gwen said. There was a slight burning sensation on her right hand for a brief moment, then it was gone. Unlike her experience with the lightning, nothing else happened. She'd feared that she would be sucked into the ground or something similar, but there was only peace and tranquility. She opened her eyes and saw Virion staring at her. Although she knew he couldn't see, it made her feel awkward.

"What does the rune do?" Gwen asked.

"It attunes you to nature. Do you see that vine?" Virion pointed at one that was dried out. "It is on the verge of death. Help it flourish once more."

Gwen wondered how Virion knew the vine was damaged if he couldn't see. Instead of keeping it to herself, she voiced her question.

"Simply because I cannot see with these eyes, does not mean that I am blind to everything," Virion said. "I am in tune with the life forces around me and can feel when they are troubled."

"You must see the world in a very beautiful way," Gwen replied. She knelt and placed her hand gently under the wilted vine. The pulse of magic in her new rune made her fingers twitch and she tried to hold them still. She licked her lips and spoke the rune.

"*Saol.*"

A surge of green energy flowed from her palm into the vine. Gwen's eyes widened in surprise. The energy tingled as it left her skin. The vine accepted the flow and its color slowly began to return. After a few more moments, the vine lifted off her hand and Gwen stopped the magic. She stood and looked at Virion.

"How does the rune restore life?" she asked.

"It doesn't restore life," Virion corrected. "Not in the way you think. Magic is in all things, but not all things can use it. When you channel the magic, it can invigorate things that have been lost. The vine was not yet dead. If it had been, the magic would not have done anything to help it. Magic can restore, and in rare cases create, but it cannot bring life to the dead."

"You said that you wanted this rune to balance me. Are you expecting me to use this rune to heal every wilting flower and tree I encounter?"

"Of course not," Virion replied. "I ask only that you use it for good."

Gwen didn't understand how she could use something inherently good for anything other than that, but she kept that to herself.

"Thank you again," Gwen said.

Virion opened his mouth to reply, then paused. A shadowed look appeared on his face and his eyebrows creased in concentration. He grunted and grabbed at his side, then crumpled to the ground.

"What is it?" Gwen asked, kneeling down and gingerly touching his shoulder. "Did I do something wrong?" She feared she must have done something incorrectly with the vine.

"Something dark has tainted Auleavell," Virion said between grunts of pain.

Gwen looked back at Lyra. She motioned for Gwen to follow her.

"Do I need to get help?" Gwen asked Virion.

"I feel what Auleavell feels," he said. "I'll be fine. Go if you must."

Gwen left the garden and followed Lyra. The elven woman walked hurriedly and kept glancing around at their surroundings.

"What is it?" Gwen asked. "Virion said something tainted Auleavell. Can you feel it, too?"

"I am not as connected to this place as Virion, but I sense something is amiss."

They reached the palace tree just as Kirith was coming out. Aimil followed behind him. Kirith looked troubled. "People are getting ill," he said. "It seems to have come out of nowhere. Not everyone is being affected, but we don't know what the source is."

"Caused by people loyal to your father?" Lyra suggested.

"Maybe, but I don't believe so. My father is a hard man, but I don't think he would cause injury to his own people."

"Desperation can make people do unthinkable things," Lyra said.

Gwen felt something tugging at her mind, then pain lanced through her skin where her new rune was. She pressed her fingers to the back of her hand and suddenly she saw a vision of a river flowing underground.

"The river," Gwen said.

"The Thaestra? What of it?" Kirith asked.

"I think that's the source."

Kirith regarded her suspiciously. "What do you mean?"

Gwen lifted her hand to display the rune. "Virion gifted me with this. I think it's trying to tell me where the sickness is coming from."

"I must go and pray to Solara," Lyra said suddenly. "Forgive me, my Lord. I will find you when I am done."

Lyra rushed off and Gwen looked from Aimil to Kirith. It seemed the worst possible time to pray, but perhaps Lyra had some insight that wasn't evident to her.

"Let us go and see if the rune speaks truly to you," Kirith said.

He led them through the forest-city, heading north until they reached a large clearing. Five trees ringed the area, and between two of them was a glowing barrier. The barrier resembled a mirror, reflecting their appearances to them. Gwen tried to peer through it to see what was on the other side, but she only saw herself.

"This is the only way to the Thaestra," Kirith said. "You'll feel disoriented when you go through it, but it's only momentary." He wasted no time and stepped through, disappearing completely from view.

"Your turn," Aimil said.

Gwen stepped through and a powerful wave of nausea struck her. She staggered and almost fell, but Kirith grabbed her arm and steadied her. Aimil came through and stopped suddenly, looking past Kirith and Gwen, her mouth open in shock.

Kirith appeared confused and followed her gaze. He gasped. Gwen's queasiness subsided and she saw the startled look on Aimil's face.

"What is it?" she asked, then turned to look.

Standing beside the Thaestra River was a dragon.

CHAPTER 10

Conal

"They were looking for me?" Bryok frowned, avoiding Conal's questioning glance.

"Yeah," Seren answered. "Said you'd know where to find a dragon."

"Me?" Bryok exclaimed. "A dragon? What made them think that?"

"I know, right?" she smirked. "Like I said, they were all on the loony side."

"How about we worry about that in the morning," Conal suggested, yawning. "I'm tired."

"G'night, Boss," Seren grinned.

Tethering his horse next to Bryok's, Conal leaned in and in a tone only Bryok could hear, said, "They were looking for you. How would they know that about you?"

"I don't know," Bryok grimly replied.

"How would they know you were even here?"

"I said I don't know," Bryok snapped.

"Well you better figure out something fast, because they knew exactly where you were, where we were."

Bryok's lips pursed and he twisted his right forearm to reveal a small set of runes near his elbow. Instead of the imprinted black ink, the runes gave off a very faint shimmer of crimson.

Conal saw it. "Why does that rune look weird? Never noticed it before."

Bryok slowly shook his head, his face grim. "This has never happened before."

"What's that rune for?"

"It is a special rune, one that I will not divulge at this time," he brusquely answered. "You will find out soon enough. Get some sleep. We need to get to Pharyl by tomorrow."

Though dissatisfied with the reply, Conal knew enough not to argue. He was pleased to see that Maldwic had set up a spot for him to stretch out next to his bed roll.

"Everything OK, Boss?"

"You still awake?"

"Wanted to make sure you were OK before I settled down."

"Everything's fine. Thanks for setting up a spot for me."

"Anytime. You run into those crazy fellas, the ones about the dragon?"

"No," Conal lied. "Why'd they think we'd know anything about dragons?"

"They were looking for that half-druid."

"So I understand," he yawned. "Talk about crazy."

Maldwic uttered a soft chuckle. "Know what I think, Boss?"

"What?"

Maldwic lowered his voice. "I think they might not have been as crazy as we think."

Conal twisted his head to stare at him. "Dragons? Do you believe in dragons?"

"I've never seen one or heard of anyone that has seen one. But… that doesn't mean they might not still exist."

"So, they've been hiding all this time? Think about it. A dragon has to eat and drink. In all this time, no one has even accidently bumped into one?"

"I know, I know," Maldwic agreed. "Still… that half-druid knows something."

"What makes you say that?"

"He's a druid."

Conal turned his head to see Bryok flipping a blanket of his shoulders. "Maybe you're right. Be nice to have dragons on our side."

"Have to find them first," Maldwic said.

"True," Conal drowsily answered. "In the meantime, we have enough things to worry about."

There was a heavy pause before Maldwic asked, "Are we still highwaymen, Boss?"

"Not anymore, Maldwic. We're mercenaries now."

Maldwic pondered the change. "Seems dangerous. Not everyone is a fighter."

"Doesn't have to be. Some are planners, some are better in logistics, some might be spies and those kinds of things. However, as we add more people to our company, we might want to emphasize the fighter part."

Maldwic nodded. "And I'm still going to become the Boss?"

"Yes. I have other things I need to accomplish."

"Like what?"

"You'll find out soon enough." *And now I sound like Bryok.* "Let's get some sleep. I want to be at Denhelm by tomorrow."

"G'night Boss." Folding his hands across his chest, he was soon comfortably asleep.

Conal's thoughts wouldn't let him rest and by the time he drifted off to sleep, he felt his shoulder shaken and Maldwic grinning at him.

"Time to get going, Boss."

Rubbing his bleary eyes, Conal glanced around to see everyone else was awake, rolling up bedrolls while munching on jerky, day old bread, apples or anything else from their saddle bags. His stomach growled and he stood and stretched.

"Boss."

Conal turned and Maldwic tossed him an apple. "Thanks."

In short order, the company headed out the barbican, Conal in front, Bryok beside him. Galadyr and Torgreth had yet to settle their debate, but the topic had drifted from carvers to fighters and now to cooking. Conal wondered how soon it would touch on who were the better lovers.

The ride to Denhelm was uneventful. Conal figured the size of the company, all carrying weapons, was enough of a deterrent.

It was early evening by the time they arrived as the gate guards shooed people in or out in order to close the gates for the night. Seeing the size of the troop approaching the gates, one guard alerted the other guards who spread themselves across the opening.

"What do you want?" the guard sergeant demanded, inserting himself through two guards to stand defiantly before them. He was a middle-aged seasoned soldier with the air of one used to being obeyed.

"A place to spend the night," Conal replied with a smile. "This town does have inns, does it not?"

"Of course it does. What is your business here?"

"Not that it's any of your business," Conal coolly said, "but we are here to see Lord Pharyl."

"What do you want with him?" The sergeant folded his arms across his chest and stared at Conal.

"Like I said, it's none of your business." Conal leaned forward in the saddle. "But to assuage your inquisitiveness, send a runner to notify Lord Pharyl that Conal from Hemlyn is here to see him. I'll wait." Conal watched the man frown, deliberating on how much trouble he'd get into if he bothered the Lord versus how much trouble he'd be in if he didn't report what was going on.

Deciding instead to dodge the responsibility, he turned to one of the guards. "Get the captain."

"Ah," Conal chuckled, "let someone else take the blame. A wise decision, especially if one wants to safely move up the ranks."

The sergeant shot him guilty-as-charged sour look.

Several minutes later, the captain arrived in ill humor at being disturbed. He was a short man working his way towards plump, with an unruly shock of red hair that gave him the appearance of having just woken up.

"What goes on here?" he demanded.

"Like I told your sergeant, I've come to see Lord Pharyl." Conal waved at the company behind him. "I promise my friends will be good."

"I recognize 'im cap'n," one of the guards spoke up.

The sergeant snapped his head around to glare at the man. "Why didn't you say something?"

"You'd already sent Fergud to go fetch the cap'n."

"Well out with it, man. How do you recognize him?"

"I was with Lord Pharyl when we went to Hemlyn this last time… to collect slaves. I saw him then. He's Pharyl's man," the guard replied with a hard swallow. "He's a Cobra."

The effect was instantaneous. All those within hearing distance stiffened.

"I'm sorry," the captain said, his voice almost a grovel. "Please, please, come in." He swept his hand and bowed in a grand gesture.

"Thank you," Conal affably replied though irritated at the revelation. The way things were going, everyone would know he was a Cobra. Urging his mount forward, he led the way through the gate.

Maldwic threaded his way between the others and came up alongside Conal. "Is it true, Boss?"

"Which part?"

"Both."

Conal frowned in thought. "I *was* Pharyl's man for about half a day. My guess is that he still thinks I am. That's all about to change. And yes, I am a Cobra."

"No wonder I couldn't defeat you," Maldwic marveled.

"You're a good man, Maldwic and a far better leader than Oscon ever was. I have great plans for you."

"Yes, Boss. Thank you." Not wanting Conal see him grin with pleasure, he turned to nonchalantly gaze around at the parting crowds. Most people seemed unaffected by the visitors and simply stepped aside and went about their business. It was as he started to turn his head around to make another comment to Conal that he noticed something odd. Acting as though he hadn't noticed, he turned back to Conal and smiled. "There's at least half a dozen working their way through the crowd following alongside us, more interested than normal."

Conal smiled back. "I know. I saw them when we came into the city. Pass the word to the others." As Maldwic drifted back, Conal leaned towards Bryok and raised a hand, pointing down the street. Pretending to comment on something ahead, he said, "We're being followed, and I have a feeling they're more interested in you than the rest of us."

"I noticed," Bryok grimly answered, slipping a glance down at his arm at the shimmering rune. Abruptly halting, he slid down from his saddle.

"What are you doing?" Conal demanded.

"Harder to ambush me with an arrow," he answered.

Immediately understanding, Conal ordered everyone to remain mounted and surround the druid. Galadyr and Torgreth flanked Bryok while Maldwic and others added to the protection, causing some consternation as they took up most of the street.

Yet their quick thinking thwarted the danger, though Conal knew it was temporary. Still, despite the complaints and snide comments by the citizens scrambling out of the way, they managed to safely arrive at the barbican leading into Pharyl's castle. Once they were past the portcullis, Conal breathed a sigh of relief. Entering the courtyard, he scanned the grounds. To his surprise, Lord Pharyl, flanked by half a dozen retainers, was waiting for him at the top of the steps leading to his apartments.

"Conal," Pharyl called out with a guarded smile, watching as his courtyard filled up. "I was wondering if I was ever going to see you again."

"Lord Pharyl," Conal grinned. Twisting his head to catch Maldwic's eye, he said, "Find a place close by to stay. Let me know where. Also, see what you can dig up on those who were following us."

"Got it, Boss." Maldwic circled his finger in the air and pointed out back out through the barbican.

Once Maldwic and company headed out, Conal slid down from the saddle, handing the reigns to a stable boy.

"Let me introduce my friends," Conal grandiloquently said as three more stable boys appeared for the other two horses and Torgreth's pony. "This is Torgreth, as fine a dwarf as there ever was one."

"Ach, you're much to kind, m'Lord," Torgreth flipped a hand at him, though pleased with the compliment.

"The tall handsome elf is Galadyr, and the other handsome brooding man is Bryok, a half-druid."

They both dipped their heads in acknowledgment.

Pharyl recognized a not so subtle change in his former slave. The man appeared far too sure of himself, bordering on arrogant. He would need to be brought down a notch. Taught his place. The dwarf calling him 'my Lord' was too much. Assuming his most regal demeanor, he said, "What brings you here?"

"Urgent matters that we need to discuss in private." He started up the steps, the others in tow.

A retainer, sword drawn at his side, stepped forward to interpose himself between the ascending Conal and Lord Pharyl. Without breaking stride, Conal's fist shot out, catching the man squarely in the chest and propelling him into the air over the two startled guards behind him, who simultaneously turned their heads to follow their compatriot's rapid rise and crash onto the smooth granite stones of the portico floor.

"Hold," Bryok commanded, his hands raised, as the other guards scrambled to protect their Lord. "We are not here to harm his lordship. In fact, we come to seek his aid."

Pharyl's jaw had dropped when he saw his guard sailing overhead. He had not even seen Conal's hand move when the guard was lifted off his feet.

"Who are you?"

"I'm not one to be trifled with," Conal calmly replied. "Like Bryok said, we didn't come here to cause you harm. Matters are occurring that require your involvement. May we come in?" Conal stood two steps below Pharyl.

Pharyl frowned as he appraised the man who had so recently been a mere slave. What had happened that he now traveled with an elf, a dwarf and a druid, not to mention his own company? That alone warranted his interest. But it was Conal's overt lack of knowing his place that irritated Pharyl. He had half a mind to tell him to go bother someone else. For a moment, he regretted giving him his freedom. *Still... he did exchange his life for mine. I do owe him that.*

"Yes," Pharyl finally nodded, "come inside."

Pharyl led the way through the doors, the one retainer limping as he collected himself off the floor. Pharyl's steward joined them as they entered.

The steward was an austere man with a fawning smile reserved for his lord. "The hall is ready for you, m'Lord."

"Our discussion needs to be private," Conal reminded him.

Ignoring him, the steward addressed Pharyl. "With m'Lord's approval, I've taken the liberty of providing some ale."

"That's fine Arnel," Pharyl replied. Wanting to remind Conal who was both boss and royalty, he tersely added, "The hall will be fine."

Conal jerked to a halt, causing the retainers to awkwardly stumble to avoid bumping into him. "Lord Pharyl. What we have to say is for your ears only. I chose you because I believed that you can be trusted. If after what you've heard you decide to share it, that is your choice. However, if this is more than you can accommodate, then we will leave and see if Lord Brody is more receptible."

Pharyl bristled at the man's insolence. Whirling around, he glared at his former slave. But Conal had anticipated the man's anger.

"I am not who you think I am."

"Really?" Pharyl snidely replied. "You're not the same vagabond I found in the goal in Hemlyn?"

"No," Conal confidently answered. "I'm not the same vagabond you had branded. Because you did not know, I will not hold it against you."

"Hold it against me," Pharyl exclaimed. "Now you've gone too far."

"Before you do something stupid," Conal shot back, "you may want to hear what we have to say. I traded my life for yours once before. Will you trust me enough to listen?"

Though Pharyl scowled at him, out the corners of his eyes he caught the surprised looks of his steward and retainers. Not wanting any further revelations, he twisted his head to look at the steward. "Leave us."

The steward turned an imperious gaze at the retainers. "You will wait outside."

"You too," Conal said.

"Me?" The steward cocked an eyebrow in umbrage. "But I'm his Lord's steward."

"I know," Conal drily answered. "I don't trust you like he does."

"Go Arnel," Pharyl said.

"As you wish, m'Lord." Arnel respectfully bowed then shot Conal an evil look.

Once the room was cleared of Pharyl's men, he folded his arms and cast an imperial gaze at Conal. "Well?"

Conal smiled then turned to Bryok. "You tell him."

"As you wish, m'Lord."

"What's with this m'Lord crap?" Pharyl snapped.

Bryok stood to full height. "The vagabond you had branded just happens to be the son of King Kamron of Isentol."

CHAPTER 11

Gwen

"Holy Solara," Kirith whispered.

The dragon's head perked to the side and it spotted them. Gwen expected to die. She'd heard stories of dragons breathing fire, destroying entire towns from existence. Granted, before now, she'd always assumed they were just stories, myths even, but here was one of the legendary creatures in front of her.

It was twenty feet long from head to tail, and its silver scales glittered under the rays of sunlight that filtered through the trees. Gwen didn't realize she was holding her breath until her lungs started to burn. She exhaled softly as if any sound would bring the dragon's wrath down upon them.

"Are you going to stare at me all day?" the dragon finally asked. Its voice was deep and throaty, and the words echoed among the trees. Gwen looked at Kirith and Aimil, not sure who the dragon was speaking to. The fact it spoke at all was enough to make her question her own sanity.

"You there," the dragon said.

"Me?" Gwen asked.

"Yes, *you.* Come near."

"I think it would be best if you did what it said," Kirith said lowly.

"No," Aimil said. "Dragons are sly, dangerous beasts. We should go."

Gwen was torn on whose advice to follow until the dragon narrowed its eyes on her. She felt obligated to obey the dragon and took a few tentative steps forward.

"Closer than that," the dragon huffed. "I'm not going to eat you."

Gwen looked over her shoulder. Aimil shook her head, but Kirith was motioning for her to continue. Gritting her teeth against her anxiety, Gwen closed the distance to the river and stopped when she was standing at the bank. On the other side of the river stood the dragon. She had thought the creature was massive from afar, but now that she was standing so close, it was even larger. Its scales looked smooth and when the dragon peered down at her, Gwen saw its eyes were a brilliant shade of blue.

"What's your name?" the dragon asked.

"G-Gwen." Her voice broke as she answered and she cursed herself in her mind.

"Gwen." The dragon stared at her for a long while before continuing. "This river is the source of life for Auleavell."

Gwen looked down at the rushing water. It flowed from the north, weaving among the trees until it reached where they stood. The ground curved in a natural arch and the water disappeared underground. Gwen spotted a black liquid, thick and bubbly, on the archway. It was slowly dripping into the water. As the drops fell, the water turned dark and murky.

"What is that?" Gwen asked, wrinkling her nose as a bitter smell filled the air.

"Poison," the dragon answered. "It's fouling the river."

"Who would poison the river?"

"Who indeed? Given the events that occurred today, it was probably one of the disgraced king's supporters. This is an unimaginable crime."

"How do you know what happened?" Gwen looked up at the dragon.

"Haven't you heard the saying, 'dragons see everything'?"

"No," Gwen admitted.

"We do," the dragon said.

Gwen thought that was nonsense, but she didn't want to argue with a dragon and risk being killed, so she changed the subject. "What is your name?"

The dragon eyed Gwen warily, then said, "Venia."

"That's a beautiful name."

"Thank you," Venia preened at the compliment, standing tall and flicking her tail behind her.

"I can reach that stuff with a stick," Gwen offered, bending down to grab one from under a nearby tree. She walked onto the archway and held the stick out over the water, then moved it upward to catch the black liquid. As the liquid touched the stick, the wood sizzled and popped, then caught fire. Gwen jumped back a step, then hurriedly dipped the burning end into the river to kill the flames.

"That didn't go as planned."

"The poison has a bit of magic in it," Venia said. "Hold out your hand."

Gwen lifted her left hand.

"The other one," Venia clarified.

Gwen switched hands and Venia peered at the rune on her skin.

"You have the *Saol* rune. That can help."

"How?"

"I will teach you," Venia said. "Put your hand in the water, but not near the poison."

Gwen walked back to the bank and knelt beside the river, then lowered her hand into the water. It was cool against her skin and soothed the faint burning sensation that tingled around the rune. She watched Venia's reflection on the water's surface, admiring the dragon's beauty. The creature was obviously dangerous, yet Gwen was inexplicably drawn to the dragon.

"Channel the energy of the rune into the water and speak its name."

Venia's blue eyes seemed to glow in the reflection on the water. Gwen closed her eyes and mentally visualized the green energy that pulsed within the rune. She willed the energy from herself and glowing green tendrils snaked from her palm. She opened her eyes and saw the tendrils knit themselves together, spreading through the water and obstructing the black liquid. Pain flared through Gwen's mind and hand, but she pushed through it, refusing to give in to the discomfort.

The tendrils of green energy spun around a glob of poison, circling it until the blackness faded and the water was clean. Gwen watched as the tendrils continued from spot to spot, clearing the river of the poison, but it was taking a toll on her. Weakness was creeping into her muscles and her vision started to blur. Venia said something, but Gwen couldn't make out the words. She sounded far away. Gwen tried to cut the magic off, but it continued to pour from her into the water, ignoring her frail command.

She started to panic and pulled her hand from the water. The green tendrils weren't fazed. They continued to enter the river and destroy the poison. Gwen fell onto her back and stared up at the canopy overhead, a whirring distortion of color. She felt ill and thought she was going to vomit until darkness claimed her, sharp and sudden.

When she came to, her entire body was trembling. Venia was looking down at her. Gwen didn't consider concern to be a normal emotion for a dragon, though she didn't know what normal was anymore, but she thought that's what she saw in Venia's blue gaze.

"You're alive," Venia said, a statement more than a question.

"I am," Gwen rasped, then forced herself into a sitting position. She looked around and noticed that Kirith and Aimil were gone.

"Your friends fled in fear. You shouldn't hold any ill will against them for it. Not many have seen a dragon these days."

Gwen's first instinct was to be angry with them. The dragon could have eaten or maimed her, and her allies had left her for dead. Venia's words rang with truth, though, and Gwen dismissed her anger.

"I didn't know dragons were real," Gwen admitted. Her throat was parched and her voice sounded odd in her own ears. She looked to the river, wanting to drink of the water but unsure if it was safe.

Venia followed her gaze. "You can drink," she said.

"Did we get all of the poison out?"

"Most of it," Venia answered. "You pushed yourself hard, perhaps too hard. The magic could have drained your life."

"But it didn't," Gwen said, then crawled to the edge of the bank. She cupped her hands and dipped them into the water and drank her fill, then turned her attention back to Venia. "What about the rest of the poison? Do you want me to try again?"

"No," Venia replied. "What remains will be washed away. You have done a great service for Auleavell. Not many would risk their life for a stranger, yet you risked yours for many. Perhaps there *is* hope, after all."

"Hope for what?"

"For this world. The darkness of Isentol grows daily and there are few who stand against it."

"I'm with the rebellion," Gwen said. "We're working to remove Torian from the throne. As long as there is someone fighting against tyranny, there is always hope."

"Wise words for someone so young." Venia stared intently at Gwen for a moment. "Where will you go now?"

"Aimil and I are going to Steepcross," Gwen said. "I go to learn my true name."

"The Great Library," Venia said. "I know the place, though I have not seen it in many years. The librarians are guardians of ancient tomes of power, as well as the world's history. You may be surprised at what you learn while you are there."

Venia's snout flared as she sniffed the air. "I must go," she said. "I will be watching you, Gwen. When the time comes to battle Torian, know that I will go with you."

Before Gwen could reply, Venia turned and vaulted herself into the air, her majestic wings carrying her into the sky. Gwen stood in place, watching until Venia's silver form was gone from her view. She left the river behind and headed back the way she had come. The barrier that protected the entrance to the river shimmered and pulsed. Gwen prepared herself as best as she could, then stepped through it.

A dizzying wave of sickness washed over her, but it wasn't as bad as the first time. Her vision cleared quickly, and Kirith and Aimil were there waiting for her.

"Are you all right?" Aimil asked. "Did the dragon curse you?"

"What? No," Gwen answered. "I'm fine."

"You spoke with the Guardian of Auleavell," Kirith said, awed. "She hasn't been seen by my people for over a hundred years. What did she say?"

"Someone poisoned the Thaestra," Gwen said. "She helped me cleanse the water. Well, most of it."

"You have been highly blessed." Kirith's wonder was still etched on his face.

"We need to get moving," Aimil said. "If we leave now, we might reach Steepcross by nightfall tomorrow."

"Are we in a rush?" Gwen asked. "I wouldn't mind staying another night here."

"As much as I would love to allow that, I'm afraid Aimil is right. There are already nervous whispers among my people that you two are responsible for poisoning the Thaestra. I know it's not true," Kirith added hastily, seeing Gwen's surprised expression. "I think it would be best for you to continue your journey, and I will work to quell the rumors."

Gwen decided Kirith made a valid point, especially since she was eager to learn her true name. "I can understand your people's fear," she said. "It's justified, though unfounded."

"Thank you," Kirith said. "I will ensure you leave well supplied."

"May I see Lyra before we go?" Gwen asked.

"Of course. I'll escort you there."

Kirith led them back to the forest-city and they stopped at the temple.

"I'll wait out here," Aimil said.

"And I shall get your supplies in order. Lyra should be inside praying to Solara." Kirith offered a bow and left.

Gwen stepped inside the temple and spotted Lyra kneeling in front of the dragon statue. She was the only one present aside from the guards outside and Gwen waited patiently for Lyra to finish her prayer. She enjoyed the peacefulness the temple exuded, and much like the water of the Thaestra, she felt renewed by it.

"Have you come to pray?" Lyra asked as she rose to her feet.

"No," Gwen replied. "I've come to say goodbye. Aimil and I are leaving."

Lyra walked along the pathway between the pews and joined Gwen at the doors. "Auleavell is indebted to you for rescuing Kirith from the vagabonds."

"There is no debt to be paid," Gwen said. "I did what was right."

"If you say it, then it shall be so," Lyra said. "Yet, I heard that you also healed the Thaestra."

"Who told you?"

"The Thaestra did," Lyra replied. "The waters are alive as you and I are, and they speak to those who listen."

Gwen remembered the vision she'd had and realized that the river had spoken to her through the *Saol* rune. Lyra said Auleavell was indebted to her, but she felt indebted to the elves. "Thank you," Gwen said. "For everything."

"There is much more to be done if we are to defeat Torian. I will pray that Solara guides and protects you."

"I will see you again," Gwen said, but as the words left her mouth, they felt more like a question.

"The future does not reveal its secrets, but I hope we meet again."

Gwen smiled and offered a bow, then left the temple. Aimil was gone and Kirith hadn't returned yet.

She guessed that the two might have slipped away to enjoy each other's company again, but Aimil stepped into view from the side of the temple. She hopped over a large tree root and something shiny fell into the shrubbery.

"I hope you like cheese," Kirith said cheerily as he returned. His sister was with him, carrying two leather sacks. "Your horses seem eager, too."

Gwen had almost forgotten about the horses. She was glad they wouldn't have to travel on foot. While Aimil talked with Kirith, Gwen walked over to where Aimil had dropped something and spotted a glass vial. She picked it up and was about to tell Aimil she had dropped it when she spotted what was inside. It was almost empty, but there were a few drops in the bottle and the liquid was unmistakable. She quickly stuffed the vial into her waistband and covered it with her shirt.

Aimil wasn't acting any differently, but Gwen now knew who had poisoned the river.

CHAPTER 12

Conal

Pharyl stared at Bryok, waiting for the punchline. When none came, he deadpanned, "You're serious."

"As a heart attack," Torgreth chimed in with a snort. "I know. Took me a while to get used to it. He such a loveable oaf, but it's true."

"Which brings me to another point," Bryok elaborated. "You may have unwittingly triggered the prophecy."

"What prophecy?" Pharyl asked, suddenly apprehensive.

"The eagle will bear the vipers in its claws, yet from the west a cobra will rise and strike down the eagle."

"How was I to know?" Pharyl blurted. "Are you sure he's the one?"

"Beyond all doubt," Galadyr said, not totally convinced himself, though there was something different about Conal that made him want to believe.

"How is this possible?" Pharyl argued. "He's from Urve. I remember him telling me that. Said he spent his whole life there."

"He and his sister were secreted out of Havengarde when they were quite young," Bryok explained, "during the turmoil when Torian killed Kamron. Do you remember Torian sending messengers looking for traitors to the crown, supposedly traveling with two

121

children, one a babe and the other perhaps a year older? You had just assumed the demesne here."

Pharyl blinked at the recollection. An emissary from Torian had arrived at Rexfyrd demanding Caldyr turn over any citizens of Isentol who had recently entered the kingdom, especially those traveling with two children under the age of two. To his credit, Caldyr told the emissary to "Get the hell out of my kingdom."

"I do vaguely remember that," he acknowledged.

"What Torian failed to perceive," Bryok said, "was that the children were split up. Conal went to Urve and his sister somewhere else. As time went on and his searching proved unsuccessful, he shifted his attention to his true desire – subjugating the surrounding kingdoms: elf, dwarf, and human. He has patiently gathered an army of wizards and mages to his cause. When he unleashes his forces, kingdoms will fall, one by one. Tir Manach will not be spared."

Bryok looked back over his shoulder, making sure the door remained closed. Turning back, he continued. "However, much to his shock, he recently discovered that both children live. To Conal's good fortune, Torian never suspected that he would end up with a bunch of highwaymen. However, his agents are again looking for his brother's children. In Conal's case, Torian discovered his family in Urve. That Conal never told them where he was is the only reason he is still alive."

"But it didn't save my family," Conal said through clenched teeth.

Bryok solemnly nodded. "Torian knows the prophecy. He knows Conal still lives. We believe that his sister is also alive. We have friends looking for her.

That said, it is imperative that we gain Caldyr's support to stop Torian."

Chagrined, Pharyl stared at Conal. "I... I didn't know."

"Of course you didn't," Conal said, placing a hand on Pharyl's arm. "Even I didn't know."

Pharyl's first instinct was to yank his arm away and castigate the offender, but he remembered he was now dealing with a potential king.

"We need to focus," Galadyr interrupted. "Time is of the proverbial essence."

"He's right," Torgreth added. "We got to get to Caldyr, and we need to protect him in the process." He hooked a thumb at Conal. "Though if you've ever seen him fight, you might think he don't need our help."

Conal frowned and cocked his head to stare at Pharyl. "Whatever happened to Blayne?"

Pharyl curled a lip into a snarl. "I've yet to deal with him. Brody claims ignorance yet refuses to do anything about it."

"Who's Blayne?" Torgreth asked.

"My brother-in-law's bastard son," Pharyl replied.

"He set up an ambush to kill him," Conal explained. "Didn't quite work out the way he wanted."

"Caldyr?" Galadyr reminded them. "You can deal with Blayne later."

Pharyl slid a caustic glance at him then relaxed, admitting to himself that he would deal with Blayne and Brody on his own terms... maybe even get Conal to help. "I will go with you."

"We were hoping you would say that," Torgreth grinned.

"We leave first thing in the morning," Bryok announced. "We will need a safe place to spend the night."

"You will stay here," Pharyl grandly offered, crossing the floor to open the door and curl his fingers at his steward. "Prepare lodging for our guests. Add four more places for the evening meal."

"Yes, m'Lord." Arnel dipped his head, hiding his dislike of Conal.

"I need to check on my friends," Conal stated.

"They're staying at the Stag's Head," the steward answered with an overt tone of condescension.

"And where might that be?" Conal ignored the man's conceit.

"I can have one of the servants show you," he replied without looking at him.

"How about I come with you?" Torgreth said to Conal.

"Good idea," Bryok nodded. "Galadyr and I can further enlighten Lord Pharyl."

Stepping out into the hallway, the steward address one of the servants, a young man in his early teens. Ignoring the two visitors, he commanded, "Show these two where the Stag's Head is."

"Yes, Steward Arnel." The teen reverently dipped his head.

Turning his back to Conal, the steward felt a sudden vice grip on his neck as he was physically lifted off the ground.

"The next time I come in here," Conal growled, "I expect to be treated with respect. Do you understand?"

Arnel flailed as he felt the grip tighten, and finally squeaked, "Yes."

Conal released his grip and the steward dropped to the floor and stumbled forward. Turning his back to him, Conal motioned the servant to lead the way, leaving Arnel gasping for breath.

The Stag's Head was a large respectable tavern two streets away from Pharyl's castle. When Conal and Torgreth entered, Maldwic and company had spread out and positioned themselves in strategic locations so that they could monitor who entered the tavern, who went upstairs with one of the girls, and who worked the tables, as well as keeping an eye on the taverner.

Seeing his deputy, Conal scooted the edges of other tables before pulling out a chair at Maldwic's table.

Torgreth ignored the not so subtle looks and yanked out a chair to sit next to Conal. "Think they've never seen a dwarf before," he groused.

Conal leaned back and gazed around the room, meeting the eyes of those too curious who quickly turned away. Shifting his attention back to Maldwic, he asked, "Find out anything?"

"Nuthin' yet, Boss. I just –" Maldwic stopped as he frowned and narrowed his gaze at two men who slipped in through the front door. With a satisfied nod, he caught the attention of two attractive members of the company and ticked his head at the newcomers. Immediately understanding, the two women got up from their table and started edging their way over to where the two men sat at a table near the far wall.

Conal nonchalantly leaned back, his gaze sweeping the room, lingering briefly on the two men. He recognized the one. Leaning forward, he lowered his voice. "Let me know what you find out. See how many others there are."

"You stayin' the night at Pharyl's?"

"Yes. He and I still have a lot more to discuss. We leave first thing in the morning."

"We'll be ready."

"You do realize when they see me leaving they're gonna know something's up," Torgreth pointed out, scooting his chair back.

Maldwic shot a glance over at the two women who were amiably chatting with the two newcomers whose rapt attention was focused nowhere else. He motioned to another company man, a stout man with full beard, who came to the table. "Escort our dwarf friend to the door."

"Let me know if you find out anything. Otherwise, I'll see you in the morning." Conal stood and together with the stout man, they blocked the view of the newcomers as they escorted Torgreth to the door.

Once outside, Conal scanned the streets, noting the usual bustle of merchants returning home, revelers heading to another pub, and the street urchins darting in and out among the crowd, begging for coins or racing away after failing to snatch a man's purse. What surprised him was the absence of soldiers or other security until he noticed a man standing near the street corner, pretending to be waiting for someone, a nondescript man who took more than a passing interest in them.

Catching the man's eye, he gave him a half-smile before crossing the street to head towards Pharyl's castle. The man immediately gave up pretense and openly followed them. Conal slowed his pace, causing the man to likewise slow his pursuit. Abruptly turning the corner, he grabbed Torgreth and shoved him against the building wall, placing a finger to his lips before sticking a foot out just as the man raced around the corner to catch up.

The man sprawled headlong onto the street. Conal was on him before he had a chance to react, reaching under his armpit and jerking him to standing.

"Looking for me?"

The man squinted at him, his eyes momentarily glassy as though having imbibed too much. A moment later they cleared. "Uh, no, no," he stammered. "I... I thought you were someone else. My apologies. An honest mistake. So sorry to have troubled you." He tried to escape, but Conal's grip was too strong. "You're hurting me," he whimpered as he squirmed.

"You were following me when I came into the city," Conal said, smiling with only his lips. "Why?"

"I thought you were someone else. Honest."

In one quick motion, the man lifted a knee up and pulled a stiletto out from inside his boot. But Torgreth's hand was quicker and the dwarf's grip, firm from years of carving stone, grasped the man's wrist with such strength that the stiletto dropped from his hand.

"Now that wasn't nice," Conal chided, looking down at the blade. "And here I thought we were going to be such best friends." Conal's other hand went for the man's throat and the man started gasping, feeling suddenly weak as Conal squeezed the carotid arteries. "I'll ask you one last time, why were you following me?"

The man's eyes bulged as he struggled to pry Conal's fingers from his throat. "Not... you," he rasped.

"Who?"

"Other... man," he slurred.

Conal felt him weakening and he relaxed his grip. "Why?"

Gasping for breath, the man stared defiant eyes at him. "He knows why."

"Tell me."

"He knows why," he stubbornly repeated.

"Boss," Maldwic called out, coming around the corner. "Need help?" He had two others from the company with him, a man and a woman.

"Just trying to determine why he was following us." He released the grip at the man's throat.

Maldwic scrutinized the man, narrowing his gaze at him. "You got some friends of yours in the Stag's Head?"

The man swallowed and nodded.

Maldwic rolled his eyes and shook his head, letting out a huff of exasperation. "He's one of them."

"Them?" Torgreth repeated.

"They're dragon hunters," Maldwic scoffed.

"Dragon hunters?" Conal pushed the man away from him. "By the gods, you idiot." He jabbed a finger into the man's chest. "You tell those clowns that if I see any of you fools following us or interfering with us, I will track you down and rip your throats out myself."

The man's hands went to his throat and before anyone could stop him, he scampered off like a frightened rabbit.

"What is wrong with people," Conal snarled.

"I know," Maldwic chuckled.

"Keep an eye out," Conal said. "If they get in the way, we take them out."

"Why?" Maldwic asked, surprised. "They're harmless."

Conal remembered the fight in the forest clearing when Krag escaped just in time. "I don't want them tailing us or compromising us," he explained. "We don't need their crazy notions. You know as well as I do that crazy people are unpredictable."

"You are so right, Boss. Had an aunt once that was crazier than a cross-eyed smithy. Don't know what happened to her, but I always kept my distance"

Conal grinned and placed a hand on his shoulder. "Once we get things better settled, I'll bring you into the planning sessions. Right now, I'm having to flatter and grovel more than I can stand."

Maldwic laughed. "I understand, Boss. We'll be ready."

"I know you will. That's why, as of this moment, the company is yours."

Startled, Maldwic's chest puffed up. "Thank you, Boss. I won't let you down."

"I know. See you tomorrow morning."

"Right, Boss."

There were guards at the gate when Conal and Torgreth approached Pharyl's castle. Upon seeing Conal, they snapped to attention.

"Good evening, Sir," one guard said, staring directly at Conal, causing him to wonder at the overly polite and respectful greeting.

"Good evening," Conal replied.

"What? No 'good evening' for me?" Torgreth quipped.

"Uh," the guard sputtered and swallowed. "Yes, uh, yes... sir. Good evening."

"That's more like it," Torgreth smirked.

They found Bryok and Galadyr still in the Great Hall with Pharyl. Pharyl looked up when they entered. Upon seeing Conal, he crossed the floor to greet him.

"I believe I owe you many apologies, m'Lord."

Caught off guard at the change, Conal shot a look at Bryok who nodded that all was well. "None needed, Lord Pharyl. Neither of us knew. However, that was then. We need to convince Caldyr to help us."

"Lord Pharyl has offered half his army for our cause," Galadyr said.

"Half? That is very generous."

"I believe it is necessary," Pharyl said, with an air of self-importance. He would have to get used to treating this youngster with respect, awkward as it might prove to be. "My army commander should be here any moment."

"Thank you," Conal replied as regally as possible. "Bryok. Might I have a word with you?"

Bryok frowned with a quizzical look then joined Conal as he walked to a corner of the large hall.

"Your arm," Conal said.

Bryok cast a surreptitious glance to where Pharyl and Galadyr chatted before turning back to Conal. He lowered his voice and pointed to his forearm. "It glows and I feel a slight burn."

"Those who followed us are dragon hunters, but then you already knew that, didn't you," Conal challenged.

"Yes."

"Are you going to tell me what's going on? Like last time, they knew you were here."

"I don't know how," Bryok answered through gritted teeth, "though that's not entirely true."

Conal said nothing, waiting for him to continue.

"No doubt all the hunters are rune-marked. My guess is that they are rune-bound to Torian or one of his wizards." He locked Conal with a cold hard stare.

"They must receive no mercy, for they will never give any."

"So you're saying…"

"Yes." Bryok added a curt nod. "When we find them, we must kill them."

CHAPTER 13

Gwen

After leaving Auleavell, Gwen and Aimil rode until evening and then set up camp on the side of the road. The landscape was a long stretch of flatlands comprised of tall golden grass that swayed in the breeze. They ate a small meal from the supplies Kirith had given them, and Aimil offered to take the first watch.

Gwen laid on the ground and stared up at the night sky, counting the stars and trying not to think about her earlier revelation. Aimil had dropped a vial that contained what appeared to be the same poison that had infected the Thaestra River. Gwen was certain it was the same liquid, but she wanted to be able to confirm it. The problem was that she didn't know how. And even if she did, what could she do about it?

The most troubling thing to Gwen was *why*. Why had Aimil done such a horrid thing? It didn't make sense unless Kirith had snubbed her in some way. Even then, Gwen didn't believe that Aimil would go to such lengths. At least, she didn't want to believe the woman would do something like that. Yet, she had to consider how she barely knew the woman.

If Eradore trusts her, then so should I, Gwen thought.

She struggled with her feelings until sleep eventually claimed her. When Aimil woke her for her turn at watch, Gwen felt like she'd only just fallen asleep. She rose and tended the fire until sunrise when she allowed the embers to go cold. They ate breakfast, mostly cheese and grapes, and then rode most of the day. They stopped only a handful of times, and only long enough to relieve themselves or to allow the horses to drink.

They kept a steady pace, with Aimil determined to reach the capital city of Steepcross, called Arbington, before nightfall. When the city was finally within sight, the sun was in the middle of the sky. Gwen was surprised at how quickly they'd arrived. Large braziers stood outside the gates to light the way for straggling travelers, but they were empty now. The guards at the gates were dozing at their posts and Gwen and Aimil entered the city without issue.

"The Great Library requires an appointment, so we'll bide our time at the Crow's Foot," Aimil said, guiding her horse along the main cobbled street. "I've stayed there before. It'll do for our needs."

"What about our horses? Will the Crow's Foot board them?"

"No, we'll have to leave them somewhere else, but I know just the place."

Aimil led the way through the city, keeping to the main streets until they reached the other end of the city where another gate, this one smaller than the main one, led out into the countryside. The area was quiet, but a pungent smell lingered in the air.

"Most of the stables are located in this part of the city," Aimil said. "It keeps the stench and the mess in one place."

"That's a good idea," Gwen replied. "Having to smell this," she waved her hand, "while eating or drinking in a tavern would be less than ideal."

"Exactly. It also provides an easy exit if we have to leave quickly."

Gwen wondered why they might have to make a hasty retreat, but she said nothing. Every little thing Aimil said came across as suspect now that she'd found the vial. They left the horses with a young boy and paid the boarding fee to an older man whom Gwen assumed was the boy's father.

Aimil and Gwen backtracked to the center of the city and entered a large building with a sign that hung from the roof that read *Crow's Foot*. Gwen felt more at home than she had in weeks. The inn was crowded and a troupe of musicians was playing a lively tune. The atmosphere was one of camaraderie and the ale was flowing. Gwen found it all refreshing and allowed herself to forget her problems for a while. She was so enrapt with the music that she barely heard Aimil say she was going to get them an appointment at the Great Library.

Gwen was pleasantly surprised when she spotted a familiar face. A young man was moving through the crowded room, making his way to where the musicians were. Brown hair, clean-shaven, handsome.

It was definitely him.

He waited for the troupe to finish their final song, then took their place and struck up a tune with his lute. Gwen watched him intently, remembering his performance from the last time she saw him. That had been the night that started it all and had put Gwen on the path to joining the rebellion. The bard's fingers strummed over the strings, playing with practiced ease. He was just as good as she remembered. She smiled, happy to know that he'd escaped her father's inn and that nothing ill had befallen him. Other memories, darker ones, hovered at the edge of her mind, but she kept them at bay by focusing on the music.

Aimil eventually returned and sat across from Gwen. The bard played several more songs before another musician took over, and then Gwen turned her attention to Aimil.

"How did it go?"

"As well as can be expected for a last-minute request," Aimil replied. "But one of the librarians owes me a favor, so I was able to get us in. If you're done drooling over the handsome bard, we can go now."

"I wasn't—" Gwen sputtered.

"Whatever," Aimil interrupted. "Are you ready to go? We've got a limited amount of time inside."

Gwen rose from her seat. "I'm ready."

Despite her tone of confidence, she had a lot of trepidation about learning her true name. Tobias had once mentioned that he thought she was the lost princess of Isentol, but she doubted that was true. And while Boris had admitted that he wasn't her real father, she didn't think that meant Tobias had been right.

They left the Crow's Foot and headed west toward a stone structure that Gwen had mistakenly assumed was a castle. It was plain and unadorned. A moat surrounded the building and the two women had to cross a bridge to reach the grounds of the Great Library. The entrance wasn't guarded, but there were two great wooden doors that Gwen thought would be impossible to move without a small army.

Aimil knocked on one of the doors. A few moments passed, and then a small rectangular panel slid open and two eyes peered out.

"Yes?" It was a woman's voice. Gwen thought she sounded old, perhaps someone of sixty or seventy years.

"We have an appointment," Aimil answered.

The eyes shifted from Aimil to Gwen, then the panel slid shut and the door opened. Gwen had been right. The woman standing before them was in her later years. Her hair was long, gray mingled with white. Her skin hung loosely on her face and she wore a flowing blue robe trimmed in silver.

"Very well," she said, stepping aside. "Speak your name and enter."

"Aimil Cirillo." Aimil stepped forward and crossed the threshold of the doorway.

"Gwen Wilmarth." Gwen stepped forward, hoping she didn't experience a wave of nausea like she had in Auleavell. To her surprise, an invisible barrier kept her from entering the library.

"Try it again," the old woman said. "And use your true name this time."

"That is my name," Gwen replied.

She cleared her throat and said her name again, louder this time. When she tried to enter the library, she was again held back by the invisible force. Aimil was smirking, but the old woman frowned and eyed Gwen suspiciously.

"Deception will not gain you access into the library."

"I'm being truthful," Gwen protested. "That is my name."

"No, it isn't," the woman said. "Else the ward would have let you in."

"I can vouch for her," Aimil chimed in. "She's a new mage, and it's possible her given name at birth isn't the same one she has today."

The old woman pondered over the information for a moment, then said, "I've heard of stranger things happening before." She snapped her fingers and traced a symbol in the air with her hand. There was a sound of rushing air, then the old woman motioned for Gwen to come inside.

Gwen hesitantly stepped forward and this time she wasn't hindered. The temperature in the library was noticeably colder than outside, and the smell of old parchment filled Gwen's nostrils.

"It seems you need to learn your true name," the woman said.

"Yes. That is why I have come here."

"I see. You could have said that to begin with. Follow me."

The woman led the way through the library, which appeared much larger from the inside than Gwen would have imagined. There were dozens of rooms down various hallways, and books were everywhere.

"I'm the Head Librarian," the woman said as they walked. "My name is Marjorie, but you will call me librarian while you are here."

"Thank you for seeing us on such short notice," Gwen said.

"I don't make the schedule, dear, I just adhere to it."

"Does the title Head Librarian mean you are over this entire place?" Gwen asked.

"In a manner of speaking," Marjorie answered. "Though we have the Council of Librarians, and we all collectively make decisions by a majority vote."

"They are also all wizards like Eradore," Aimil said.

"A common fact," Marjorie said. "We consider ourselves a magocracy, if you will."

"A what?" Gwen asked.

"Leadership run by wizards," Marjorie clarified.

"I thought wizards were rare?"

"We are. This is probably the only place you'll ever see more than two wizards together outside of the Chamber of the Altar. Though if the rumors are to be believed, King Torian has negated the treaty with the Order and his guards have barred access to the Obsidian Altar."

"It's true," Gwen said. "I was there when they cleared the place out."

Marjorie huffed under her breath, clearly upset by the news. She turned right down a hallway and stopped outside one of the doors. Reaching into her robes, she withdrew a brass key and slid it into the lock, turned it, and hid the key back within her robes.

"This room holds the Stone of Truth," Marjorie said. "It is here where your true name shall be revealed." Marjorie pushed the door open and stepped into the room, then closed it once Gwen and Aimil had entered.

Gwen expected something grandiose, like a giant diamond or some other precious stone. Instead, there was a wooden table that held a palm-sized violet-blue colored stone. It was smooth and polished. Gwen wasn't certain, but she thought the stone was giving off a faint light.

"I've never seen anything like that before," Gwen said softly.

"It's an azurite stone," Marjorie replied. "It's imbued with ancient magic, spells older than the Great Library itself. Some say it was given to wizards by the goddess Solara."

"I can believe that," Gwen said.

"I wouldn't," Aimil rolled her eyes. "Solara is a myth."

"Have you ever seen Solara?" Marjorie asked, looking at Aimil.

"No."

"Have you ever been beyond the horizon, to the land of the Godhood?"

"Of course not," Aimil replied. "No one has."

"Then you should not dictate to another whether something is true or not. You shouldn't make absolute statements without absolute proof. This is a place of learning, and I will not tolerate half-truths."

"Fair enough," Aimil said, but Gwen could tell she didn't like being told what to do.

"Now then, you will hold the stone and connect your *bunús* to it, then speak your name. If you are lying, you will know. Set the stone down on this parchment." Marjorie slid a fresh sheet from a stack to the center of the table. "The truth will be revealed."

Gwen swallowed the lump in her throat and reached for the stone. She could feel magic radiating from it. The energy pushed against her hand, though Gwen couldn't actually see anything. She lifted the stone and held it in her palm, then closed her eyes and envisioned the *bunús* rune in her mind. She felt it join the stone, the force of the connection almost causing her to drop it.

"Gwen Wilmarth," Gwen said.

A shock ran up the length of her arm and she cried out in surprise and pain. Gwen opened her eyes and hurriedly set the stone onto the parchment, then massaged her arm with her left hand.

"The stone knows truth from deceit," Marjorie said.

The paper hissed as the stone burned something into it, small tendrils of smoke rising into the air before quickly fading. Marjorie removed the stone and looked at the parchment.

"What does it say?" Gwen asked eagerly.

"See for yourself." Marjorie held the parchment up.

In a graceful, flowing script was the name Quinlee.

"Quinlee?" Gwen's face scrunched in displeasure. "What kind of name is that?"

"A rare name," Marjorie said, her expression curious. "There's only one person I've ever known to have it."

"Who?" Gwen asked.

"The lost princess of Isentol."

CHAPTER 14

Conal

Employing the benefits of his stealth rune, Conal lowered himself over the walls of Pharyl's castle, pausing to get his bearing. Though late, he knew the Stag's Head would still be busy. Slipping through the streets, he stood outside the tavern and listened to the cacophony of patrons enjoying another ale.

The door opened and light spilled out along with two revelers who, upon seeing Conal, greeted him as a long-lost friend. Giving them an affable grin and slap on the back, Conal brushed past them and into the tavern, rapidly scanning the room, surprised that Maldwic was still there. To his credit, the new leader of Oscon's company was sober and alert, immediately noting the new arrival. Conal weaved around the tables to finally scoot a chair out next to Maldwic.

"Surprised to see you here, Boss," Maldwic smiled.

"Surprised to see you still here, too." Conal returned the smile.

"We've tracked down four of them," Maldwic said, getting to the reason he believed Conal was here.

"Good. I've got one more job for you."

"Whatever you need, Boss," Maldwic confidently answered.

"Kill them."

While the smile on Maldwic's lips remained, what was in his eyes vanished. "Uh… we… uh, I mean I…

you know we don't have people who are good at that. We rob and steal, but we don't kill. We have a few who are capable of cold-blooded murder, but I don't completely trust them."

"I understand," he nodded. "That was one of the things I liked about the group. We were motivated by greed, not violence. I expect to use those skills in the future. As for now, tell me where they are, and I'll take care of business myself."

"No, Boss," Maldwic quickly reconsidered. After all, he was in charge now. "I'll take care of it."

"You sure?"

"Like I said, we got a couple of folks who will be more than willing to satisfy their bloodthirst. Leave it to me."

"Thanks. I'll see you in morning."

Morning came way too early for Conal. Making use of his stealth skills, he had prowled the streets until the early morning hours, noting the only people out were burglars. Twice he had come upon thieves in the process of breaking into a home. Twice he had foiled the act by remaining in the shadows and gently coughing, scaring the intruders half to death and causing them to bolt. It had been great fun; but now he was paying the price for his late-night escapade.

"Pharyl is sending a cohort of his soldiers with us," Bryok announced over a breakfast of roasted venison, fresh bread, cheese and ale. Peering intently at him, he suppressed a smile. "You look tired."

"Busy night," he said, uttering a drawn-out sigh.

"That's what you get for staying out late and partying." Bryok chuckled at Conal's confused frown. He held his forearm out to show Conal that the runes were not glowing. "Thank you."

Conal immediately understood, silently thanking Maldwic for solving the problem.

"'bout time you got up," Torgreth greeted him as he and Galadyr entered into the dining hall. He cut two slices of cheese, offering one to Galadyr. "Pharyl's cohort is about ready."

"How many are there?" Conal stood, casting a wistful glance at the unfinished breakfast.

"Slow down," Torgreth advised with a grin. "I said 'about ready,' which means another half an hour. Finish your lunch."

"Very funny," Conal smirked as he sat and ripped off a chuck of bread, slathering it with warm butter. "How many?"

Torgreth shrugged. "Didn't bother to stop and count."

Lord Pharyl strode in, his usual arrogance forcibly suppressed. "My Lord Conal. I'm sending a cohort of my best with you. I had my steward compose a missive to Caldyr, urging him to action." With an overt flourish, he produced a sealed letter, placing it on the table.

"Thank you," Conal nodded, affecting as regal an air as possible. He blinked, thinking how stupid he must have sounded. Hoping no one noticed, he shifted a glance at Torgreth whose smirk said he too thought it was rather pompous. *Good ol' Torgreth. He's the one person I can trust to tell me when I'm getting too full of myself.*

'I believe they're about ready," Pharyl said, referring to his cohort. He was ready to be rid of his guests and the sooner they were gone, the sooner he could stop pretending to fawn over this upstart.

Once outside, Conal scanned the assembled troops, his eyes lighting on Maldwic who was hustling over towards him.

"Morning, Boss," he smiled then leaned in so only Conal could hear. "Took out most of 'em last night. One managed to escape. Sorry."

"Nothing to apologize for," Conal reassured him then placed a hand on Maldwic's shoulder. "Just thankful I've got someone here I can trust." He shot a meaningful glance at the assembled cohort.

"Good morning, my Lord," the cohort commander called out as he approached. He was a wiry muscular man adorned with breastplate and carried a feathered helmet in the crook of his arm. A short sword slapped at his thigh as he walked. He was clean shaven with short dark auburn hair. "I am Cadfyn."

"Good morning, Captain," Conal amiably replied. "You have met Maldwic, chief of these marauders?"

"I have not, m'Lord," he answered, giving Maldwic a reserved nod. "I am unfamiliar with your group."

"We like to keep it that way," Maldwic said with a polite smile.

"Are we ready, Captain?" Conal interrupted before Cadfyn could probe further.

"Yes, m'Lord."

"I want to get to Rexfyrd as quickly as possible. Your cohort will take the lead. Set a good pace."

"As you wish, m'Lord." He saluted and jogged over to where his orderly held his mount.

"I want you close by," Conal whispered to Maldwic. "Not that I don't trust the man... I just like having a more responsive force close by."

"You expecting trouble, Boss?"

"Not sure. Let's just say I have a feeling."

Conal's jitters proved unfounded as the first day's travel proved quite uneventful. They camped outside the small town of Athgal, two hours travel beyond the border of Pharyl's demesne. At first the town's sole tavern was thrilled to have the increase in business. That lasted until just before the ale ran out when two of Captain Cadfyn's soldiers got into a shoving match that turned into a brawl, which ended up destroying most of the furniture inside the pub.

Things didn't get any better when Conal and Bryok were awoken in the middle of the night by the tavern owner who demanded immediate payment.

More than cross because he hadn't slept much the night before, Conal, along with Bryok, confronted Cadfyn who seemed unaffected by the destruction.

"They're just letting off some steam, m'Lord. You know how it is."

"Letting off steam," Bryok snapped. "They destroyed the man's pub. Are you going to pay for the damages?"

"I gave the man a chit in Lord Pharyl's name. He'll get paid," Cadfyn replied, wondering why they were so irritated.

"Paid? And how long will that take?"

Cadfyn shrugged. "Don't know. Not my problem anymore."

"Are you that stupid?" Bryok burst. "How is he supposed to gain support if you're destroying everything in the process?" He thrust a finger at the indignant pub owner who stood close by. "What will he tell King Caldyr when word gets out that the army marching through here destroyed his business?"

"He'll get paid... probably a whole lot more than the pub's worth. The way I see, he's come out better in the long run."

"Really?" Conal interjected. "When do you think Lord Pharyl will deliver good on *your* promise? Your soldiers caused the damage; your soldiers can pay for the damage."

Cadfyn blinked in surprise. "I don't think that's a good idea. If they spend their money now, they won't have enough for when we get to Rexfyrd."

"That's not my problem," Conal shot back, amazed at the man's stubborn stupidity. "No one is going anywhere until you have given this man satisfaction."

"With all due respect, my Lord," Cadfyn retorted, his voice dripping contempt, "I take my orders from Lord Pharyl. His orders were to escort you to Rexfyrd. What happens along the way with my soldiers is my concern, not yours."

Conal noted disrespectful use of 'm'Lord' in addition to the man's insolence. His face hardening, he narrowed a penetrating gaze at Cadfyn. "You are of no use to me. Take your ill-disciplined rabble and go back. I no longer have any need of you."

Cadfyn stiffened, standing to full height. "I repeat; I take my orders from Lord Pharyl."

A sudden premonition flooded within Conal. Controlling the urge to teach the man a lesson, he shook his head, spun around and marched off.

Startled, Bryok chased after him. "That's not the way to settle this. You need to show him who is in command here."

"I know," Conal answered in a hushed voice, stepping close to an unattended campfire. Pulling out the letter Pharyl gave him for Caldyr, he glanced up at Bryok then slid a finger under the envelope flap and broke the seal. Pulling the letter out, he flipped it open when a smaller folded piece of paper slipped out. He caught it midair. Tilting the larger letter to read it by the firelight, he scanned it then quietly read it aloud to Bryok.

My Lord Caldyr,

The bearer of this note is a man claiming to be the son of King Kamron. The friends he has with him will stubbornly vouch for this claim. I confess that, despite the clever story they've conjured, I cannot bring myself to believe a word of it. All to recently I had purchased this man as a slave and had him branded. Determining that he demonstrated an unusual level of intelligence, I decided to manumit him and retain his services. Events occurred where he was detained by highwaymen and I lost the use if his abilities. Imagine my surprise (and humor) when he showed up claiming to be a king's son

He likewise claims that Torian is plotting to overthrow Tir Manach and it is his intent to prevent Torian from accomplishing these supposed plans. I would normally assume these the rantings of a madman and would have imprisoned him here but thought you might enjoy a good diversion. I send him with an escort of soldiers under the command of Captain Cadfyn. Cadfyn is not the sharpest blade in the armory, but he is obedient to a fault.

One additional matter needs to be brought to your attention and that is the presence of dragon hunters. I was more than surprised to discover the presence of at least a half-a-dozen of these strange individuals. Why they are here and now truly baffles me. I have questioned several of them and their response is uniform – the dragons have returned. I have one or two under surveillance but view them for the present as harmless fools. Still, I thought it might interest you.

Your obedient servant

Pharyl

Conal glanced up at Bryok. "Skillfully done. I carry the letter condemning me."

"What's the other one say?"

Conal unfolded the small page. The handwriting was tight and neat.

My King,

In accordance with your wishes, I submit my observations concerning Lord Pharyl's letter. The gist of his letter is correct. This individual named Conal is an arrogant huckster pawning an unbelievable fable. He has even hoodwinked an elf, a dwarf and a druid with his outlandish tale. He should be dealt with as your wisdom decides.

As to the matter with Brody's son Blayne, it is as Your Highness surmised. How Lord Pharyl managed to escape is certainly cause for consideration.

One further point - I do not trust the druid.

Your humble servant,

Arnel

Conal sighed in disgust. "And to think that I trusted Pharyl. The steward's an ass, so it's to be expected. But I really thought Pharyl was on our side."

"Interesting that Pharyl's steward is reporting back to the king," Bryok observed.

"What should I do with these?"

"Burn Pharyl's and save the steward's letter. It might prove useful later on." Bryok turned to glance back over his shoulder to where Cadfyn strutted with self-importance, having frog-marched the proprietor back to town with the threat of physical harm should he continue his harangue. "We need to jettison ourselves from this excess baggage."

"I agree. How? It's not like we can just sneak away. He's got his security out patrolling the area." Conal tossed Pharyl's letter onto the fire, watching the paper curl as it burned. "We need a diversion, something to keep them occupied enough for us to break away." Movement to the right caught his eye and Maldwic emerged from the darkness with a man Conal did not recognize.

"Hey, Boss, Bryok," Maldwic nonchalantly greeted them. "Want you to meet a new friend of mine. Goes by the name of Lorkan. Thought you might find what he has to say very interesting."

Lorkan was a tall muscular man dressed as a woodsman, bow in hand and a quiver of arrows over his shoulder. He respectfully bowed then glanced around at the surrounding campfires where Cadfyn's cohort were peacefully slumbering.

"My Lord," Lorkan said. "Do not proceed to Rexfyrd. Caldyr is under Torian's control. He has issued orders to find you."

"Who are you?" Conal demanded.

Lorkan lowered his voice. "I am a friend of Drustan. He told me to intercept you before you got to Rexfyrd."

Conal turned to Maldwic. "Do you trust him?"

"I do, Boss."

"That's good enough for me." Conal shifted his attention to Lorkan. "How did you get past security?"

"What security?" Lorkan sniffed in disdain. "I passed through the cohort soldiers unchallenged. To be fair, once I got to Maldwic's area, I was immediately challenged."

"It's not like we can just pack up and leave without being noticed," Conal pointed out.

"I believe I can help with that, m'Lord," Lorkan grinned. "If you can assemble your force to the side towards the road, I can create enough disturbance to give you a chance to escape. Head down the road to the next town. I have people there waiting for you."

"Give me five minutes."

"Yes, m'Lord." Lorkan dipped his head in respect then spun around and disappeared into the darkness.

"Why do I feel like I'm on the open sea in a boat with no rudder," Conal sighed. Inhaling a deep breath, he rubbed his tired eyes. "Guess we better wake up a dwarf and an elf."

"Already alerted them, Boss."

Conal smiled. "Why does that not surprise me."

In less than five minutes, Conal and his loyal group had stealthily edged over by the road, separating themselves from Cadfyn's cohort who slumbered fitfully, impervious to anything but their rest.

An explosion rocked the night as a blast of fire and light burst from one of the campfires followed by a voice crying out, "We're being attacked."

Shaken out of their deep sleep, most of Cadfyn's cohort scrambled out of their bed rolls, reaching for swords. Another flash of light instantly followed by another explosion erupted on the perimeter opposite Conal.

"They're here," another voice cried out.

As Cadfyn's soldiers raced across the campsite, Conal and company vanished into the darkness.

CHAPTER 15

Gwen

Gwen stared at the name on the parchment.

Could it be true? Had Tobias been correct in his guess about her heritage? No, it couldn't be. Yet here was a sliver of proof.

"I …" Gwen didn't know what to say. Words and concise thoughts eluded her.

"Take a deep breath," Marjorie said. "It's not every day someone learns they are born to royalty."

Gwen nodded, trying to wrap her mind around the idea that she, a lowly barmaid, was in reality a princess.

"It's not possible," she said.

"The term would be improbable," Marjorie corrected. "Nothing is impossible, especially where magic is concerned."

"But how? Wasn't King Kamron and the queen murdered by King Torian?"

"Yes, they were." Marjorie pursed her lips, which caused her wrinkled flesh to tighten and Gwen thought she could imagine how the woman looked when she was a bit younger. "There is something I want to show you."

"What is it?" Gwen asked.

"It would be less impactful if I told you, so I will show you." Marjorie glanced at Aimil. "Unfortunately,

I will require you to refrain from following, but you are free to explore the library at your will."

Aimil shrugged indifferently. "Fine by me."

"Very well. Come along, Quinlee," Marjorie said.

"Please just call me Gwen."

The three of them left the room, and Marjorie turned to the right and continued down the hall. Gwen had to walk fast to keep up with her, which was surprising considering the old woman's age. Gwen glanced over her shoulder and saw Aimil walking in the opposite direction. It pained her to have Aimil out of her sight, but there was little choice in the matter.

"There was a sorcerer who frequented the library many years ago," Marjorie said, drawing Gwen's attention. "He was a recluse and always studied alone, spending much of his time learning herbology."

Gwen wondered where Marjorie was going with her story and assumed she was just rambling.

"Others told me he tended a garden at his home, cultivating rare herbs from across the kingdoms for his potions."

"That's interesting," Gwen said, humoring the woman.

"It's rather boring, actually," Marjorie said. "Unless you are into herbology?"

"Uh, not really."

"I thought not. Remember that I do not tolerate deceit here."

"I'm sorry," Gwen said with embarrassment.

"Forgiven. Now, where was I? Oh yes. Kha'gan went to Isentol to acquire a specific herb that only grows on the castle grounds. While he was there, Torian launched his coupe. He killed his brother for the throne." Marjorie shook her head sadly.

"I don't remember that being part of the story," Gwen said. Then again, until now, the story of Torian's betrayal had never really been important to her.

"They were siblings, yes. I think most people don't talk about it because they don't want to think that a family member could ever do something so terrible to another."

"It is hard to stomach," Gwen agreed.

"Even so, Torian took the throne by force and murdered anyone loyal to Kamron. And did you hear that Kamron's children were murdered?"

"Yes, I have heard that part of the tale before. That's wicked. And another reason why it is hard for me to believe I am Kamon's daughter." Gwen's stomach churned at the thought of someone murdering innocent children.

"I've said that I do not tolerate deceit in this library, and so I shall cast that lie from your mind. Kamron's children were *not* murdered."

"They weren't?"

"No," Marjorie said. "When Kha'gan realized what was happening, he was inside the castle proper in a guest room. He was about to flee when he heard the crying of a babe. It was your cries that stopped him in his tracks. He absconded with you and your brother."

Gwen knew the story of Torian's betrayal. Anyone not living under a rock had heard it, but it always ended with the murder of Kamron's entire family, solidifying Torian's rule and claim to the throne.

"Wait," Gwen said, suddenly realizing what Marjorie had said. "He rescued both children?"

"Indeed. You and your brother, Darrbie."

"Darrbie?" Gwen tried not to laugh, but the giggling erupted from her anyway.

"Kamron chose names that were … different, to be sure."

"I'd say mortifying fits Darrbie and Quinlee more than 'different.' I'll stick with Gwen."

"Do as you wish, but if you want to enter the library in the future, you will have to use your true name."

As they conversed, Marjorie led them down several hallways, traveling further into the depths of the library. Every time they passed another librarian, they would press their hand to their chest in reverence to Marjorie.

"Kha'gan," Gwen said, stumbling over the foreign name. "Does he still come here?"

"No," Marjorie answered. "He died a few years ago."

"Oh." Gwen felt an odd sense of loss even though she'd never met him. Well, technically she might have. Marjorie seemed so convinced that she was the princess, but Gwen still had many reservations. "He told you all of this, then?"

"Not verbally. He sent for me when he was on his deathbed and gave me a book. At first, I assumed it was

158

a collection of his potions that he wanted to leave to the library. There were some recipes in it, but more importantly, it held a detailed account of Torian's actions and Kha'gan's escape. The only thing missing was where he took you and your brother."

"Did he share that information with you?"

"He did not share that information with anyone. A few days after the coupe, Kha'gan came here, exhausted and looking like a man who'd walked over his own grave. He confirmed Torian's betrayal and said he rescued two children. When I pressed him for answers, he refused to divulge anything more."

"I wonder why he never told anyone their location?" Gwen pondered aloud. "Surely, he knew someday someone might need to know the information."

"Or he knew that someone who shouldn't have that information might come looking one day. I assume that's why he cut his own tongue out shortly after."

Gwen stopped mid-step. Marjorie paused and looked at her, noting the horrified expression plastered across her face.

"Kha'gan took that secret to his grave, and I don't envy him for the things he saw that night. Many of these books are filled with tales of heroic deeds, but Kha'gan is the only hero I've ever known. I trust that you'll treasure what he did for you and that you won't let his deed be wasted in vain."

"I have vowed to remove Torian from the throne and joined myself with like-minded company," Gwen said. "The more I learn about what happened, the more my hatred for Torian grows."

They reached the end of the hall and stopped at a door that looked identical to the one that guarded the room that held the Stone of Truth. Marjorie removed the same key from her robes and unlocked the door.

"This is where we keep our most fragile books."

Gwen followed her into the room. It was illuminated by several globes of light that rested upon pedestals every few feet. The pale light revealed the room was full of tall glass cases, all of them filled with books that looked like they would fall apart if a slight breeze rustled their pages. Marjorie walked over to one of the cases and opened it, carefully retrieving a plain leather-bound book and handed it to Gwen. The leather was worn from use, but it was in good condition compared to the other books.

"Read it," Marjorie said. "Take your time. I can't risk letting you take the book from here, so you'll need to read it in this room. There's a table over there you can use. I have a few tasks to do while I'm in here, so just call for me if you need anything."

"There is one thing I need," Gwen said. She pulled the vial from her waistband and held it out to Marjorie. "Would it be possible to figure out what was in this?"

Marjorie took the vial and held it up, peering at the small drops that remained in it. "It's certainly not good, whatever it is, but I should be able to discern the contents."

"Thank you." Gwen took the book to the table and sat down. One of the globes was placed in the center of the table, providing plenty of light to read by. She gingerly opened the book and started from the first page. It was a recipe for a healing potion. The next page had one for stomach illness. Gwen continued flipping through the pages until she found the entry she was looking for. She inhaled a deep breath and prepared herself for what she was about to learn.

In the final days of King Kamron's reign ...

Gwen read Kha'gan's firsthand account of the events that happened the night of the coupe. The details were intense and Gwen had to pause a few times to wipe the tears from her eyes. So many people had lost their lives, many more than Gwen would have imagined. Guards, servants, nobles. Anyone with strong ties to Kamron had been hunted down and murdered outright.

Many doubts were fluttering around in Gwen's mind about whether or not she was really the princess. She had the same name, but that wasn't proof she was one of the children Kha'gan had rescued. And then she read the description of the children. The girl had a birthmark on the bottom of her foot. It was a random shape, a splotch of brown on the arch.

Gwen's heart lurched in her chest. She removed her boot and twisted her foot around to look at the mark she'd seen many, many times. It was the same as Kha'gan's description. Gwen swallowed hard.

It was true.

She was the princess, Kamron's long-lost daughter. She put her boot back on and digested the revelation. Nothing about it made sense, other than Boris's admission that he wasn't her real father. Gwen continued reading. Kha'gan didn't mention who he left the children with, but he did mention that each one went to a different home.

"I have a brother," Gwen whispered. She wasn't sure how she felt about that. A swirl of emotions overcame her. She was both angry and sad at having missed out on all the time with him, yet also jealous of how his life may have been. Was he raised by a wealthy noble, living a life of splendor? She would have loved a life of pampered living.

Guilt assailed her for thinking such selfish thoughts. Boris had been a great father to her, and she had never gone without. She offered a silent apology to Boris's ghost and closed the book. Gwen sat in silence for a long while and eventually Marjorie joined her at the table.

"I'm stunned," Gwen said. "It's difficult to believe, but there are so many things Kha'gan mentions that leaves little doubt as to who I really am."

"Life is about learning who you are. Every time you think you have it figured out; you find that you've changed again. The journey of self-discovery is one that never ends."

"I have a brother somewhere out there," Gwen said, motioning to the outside world. "The chances of finding him are ..."

"Improbable," Marjorie said, smiling.

"Nothing is impossible," Gwen repeated Marjorie's earlier words. "I'll try to remember that."

"I know you have a lot on your mind now, but I must add to the burden. The vial you gave me ... where did you get it?"

"I found it in some brush," Gwen said vaguely. Until she knew for certain that Aimil was responsible, she didn't want to reveal too much to anyone. It was a possibility that Aimil had merely found the vial, but Gwen wasn't sure that was the case.

"Hm." Marjorie obviously wasn't satisfied with the answer, but she didn't press the issue. "I was able to determine what that liquid was. It's a mixture of poison and dark magic. I've seen similar poisons before, but this one was slightly different. The spells that were adhered to the liquid itself are intended to destroy. Seeing as there were only a few drops left, I must assume someone used it. I fear that whoever or whatever it touched is likely dead."

Gwen nodded and kept her expression calm, but she was losing it on the inside. Magic was involved, which proved to Gwen that Aimil had indeed poisoned the Thaestra River. Now, she just had to figure out why.

"Thank you for looking into it," Gwen said. "What did you do with the vial?"

"I disposed of it, and the poison. It was too dangerous to return it to you."

That meant the evidence was gone. Gwen would have to find another way to offer proof of Aimil's wrongdoing. On top of that, she didn't know who to report Aimil's actions to. Eradore, perhaps?

"There's one more thing," Marjorie said.

"What is it?"

"The Council wants to see you."

CHAPTER 16

Conal

Conal and company were a half hour down the road when Lorkan came riding up.

"We need to pick up the pace, m'Lord. Cadfyn finally discovered you're no longer there. He was still marshalling his cohort when we left. With your permission, I'll lead the way."

"Go ahead," Conal readily agreed, praying he wasn't being led into another problem.

An hour later, Lorkan veered off the main road onto a side road that led deeper into the forest, slowing the pace as the road narrowed and twisted. Drifting back to ride beside Conal, Lorkan raised himself up in the stirrups to look behind them. Though dark, he could make out the indistinct shapes of Torgreth and Galadyr and several others behind the dwarf and elf.

"We should be clear in a little while, m'Lord. I've a few of my friends acting as decoys. They'll lead them well past the point where we entered the forest."

"Thank you. Back to my original question. Who are you?" He yawed and rubbed his eyes.

"I am Lorkan ap Dafydd. My father was your father's exchequer. When Torian usurped the throne, he kept my father in that position up until a year ago. He was accused of treason and thrown in the dungeon. His only treason was to question Torian's choice of confidants, especially Grimmar who calls himself the Mage-breaker. The man is a liar. Once my father was arrested, my family was no longer safe. My mother and sisters fled just before Torian's thugs arrived to arrest them too. I managed to escape and joined the rebellion. That is where I met Drustan and Bryok. Drustan told me who you were."

He paused and looked directly at Conal. "I was ten years old when Torian murdered your family. When no one found you or your sister, everyone assumed you too were killed by that butcher. I can only imagine the shock that Torian suffered when he discovered you were not dead."

"Your father and your family?"

Lorkan shook his head and shrugged, gently rocking in rhythm with the horse's gait. "I do not know. I pray my mother and sisters are safe. My father?" His voice trailed off.

Conal understood. Most likely Lorkan's father was made to suffer then killed in retribution for his family's escape. Deciding to change the subject, he calculated that Lorkan was nine or ten years older than he. "You never married?"

"Torian decreed that any marital arrangement of a member of his extended court, including the children, had to have the king's approval, which usually involved a large sum of money. Add to that the directive that the king himself would arrange marriages. While that improved the prospects of the homely and awkward children, others were not as fortunate, especially those families seeking to arrange appropriate matches... or anyone wanting to marry for love."

"So you never married," Conal repeated, disgusted with the malevolence of his father's murderer... his uncle. *Torian is my uncle.* The realization startled him. Up to now, Torian was simply an evil king, a man who needed to be destroyed so that peace and order could be restored. But now... Torian was a blood relative, a close blood relative. The thought burst within that he was on a quest to kill his uncle. How was that different from a brother killing his older brother?

Conal's family in Urve crowded into his musings and he remembered the years growing up at the seaport and the unconditional love of a man and wife who placed his future above their own lives. *He didn't just kill my royal father... he killed my real father, the man who raised me and loved me. He killed my family, the only family I ever had.* Conal's resolve stiffened like cold hard granite and he understood what must be done. No quarter would be given, nor mercy offered. Like a rabid dog, the man needed to be put down.

"No," Lorkan answered.

Conal knit his brows, struggling to remember the direction of the conversation. That's what happened when he was tired and needed sleep. Thankfully Lorkan continued.

"I managed to avoid Torian's marriage entrapment. I absented myself from Havengarde by joining the army, volunteering for border security, a job few wanted."

"Why?"

Lorkan chuckled. "It's boring. Up until a year ago, just before my father was arrested, border security consisted of checking merchant wagons and chasing the occasional brigand. The rest of the time is spent dealing with pub owners complaining about soldiers damaging their pubs or bonding soldiers out of goal for drunkenness and fighting, and the occasional father threatening to kill the man who got his daughter pregnant. But truth be told, I'd rather be there than Havengarde."

"And now?"

"Now? Now I'm part of the resistance, the rebellion to overthrow Torian before he enslaves us all. The rebellion is wider spread than many realize, and I think Torian is just now recognizing it." He again turned his head to look at Conal. "That you are alive and well, and now assuming command of the rebellion gives us great hope and a fighting chance."

Conal's jaw slacked open and then immediately clamped it shut, hoping it was dark enough that Lorkan didn't see the shock on his face. *Assuming command? Me? Now?* He suddenly felt overwhelmingly inadequate. *What do I know about grand strategy or leading an army? I thought Bryok and Drustan were in charge.* Yeah, he had talked a good game with Maldwic, but now the heavy burden of leadership was dumped on him.

Then just as suddenly, confidence filled him. He could do this. He knew he had leadership talent when he had chaffed under Oscon's domineering hand. More than once he had offered a plan only to be told to shut up and remember his place and then see Oscon use his plan and claim it was his idea. He remembered the last encounter with Oscon. It had felt more than good to show the man that Conal was now in charge.

Up ahead, a man stepped out onto the path, an arrow notched in his bow. "Good morning Commander Lorkan."

"Good morning. All quiet?" Lorkan reined in his horse causing everyone else behind him to stop.

"Yes sir."

"Good. How did you know who we were?"

"We could hear you coming, Commander. By the conversation, we assumed you were talking with Prince Darrbie."

"That's Prince *Conal*," Conal sternly corrected. He shot an angry glance at Lorkan. "My name is Conal. Anyone calls me Darrbie, I'm gonna reach down his throat and rip his heart out."

"Yes, m'Lord," Lorkan soothed. "I'll put the word out."

"My apologies, m'Lord," the man said with a startled bow. "I didn't know."

"I understand." Conal turned to Lorkan. "Where are we?"

"We are at my camp, m'Lord. We are safe here. It's time for you to get some rest." He led the way past the sentries, staying on the path, the forest on both sides.

Expecting to see a campfire or two, Conal was surprised that not only were there no campfires, he couldn't tell how many were encamped. Yet the longer they plodded along, the more he wondered how large Lorkan's force was.

"How many do you have here?"

"Almost 3000."

"3000," Conal exclaimed.

"Yes, m'Lord. I know it might not seem much, but with the dwarven force under King Rorkyn and the army of King Kilmaryn, we probably have over 10,000 soldiers ready to heed your command."

Once again Conal's mouth gaped open. 10,000 soldiers submitting to his command. *By the gods, what have I gotten myself into?* Overwhelmed, fatigue flushed through him, yet he knew he had to act like a leader, even when he was bone tired.

They emerged into a small clearing and stopped before a marquee tent with scalloped edging, large enough to house four or more individuals. Lorkan dismounted and waved a hand at the tent.

"This is for you m' Lord."

"The whole thing?"

"Yes, m'Lord."

Dismounting, Conal frowned at the size of the tent. Someone had to set it up, take it down, and pack it for travel. "This is too big. Where'd you find it?"

Lorkan hid a grin. "It was… uh, donated, m'Lord."

"What about the rest of my friends?"

"They're all taken care of."

"They can stay with me."

"If that is what you wish, m'Lord."

"Where are you bedded?"

"Close by, m'Lord." He pointed to a wall tent less than half as large to the left.

Maldwic strode up, leading his horse.

"With your consent, m'Lord," Lorkan said, "I've placed your commander in this tent here." He pointed to a tent similar to his on the other side of Conal's tent.

Once the arrangements were settled and three more cots brought into Conal's tent, Lorkan bid him 'Goodnight' and went to check his security. Conal pulled the flap aside to his tent and entered, followed by Torgreth, Bryok and Galadyr.

A small brazier on a field table gave dim light to the interior where four cots with cotton stuffed mattresses on top were positioned. The sight of a comfortable bed was all Conal needed and he made a beeline to the farthest cot, sat down, yanked off his boots, and flopped back, yielding a sigh of contentment and was quickly asleep.

It was late morning when he woke, his stomach growling. Sitting up, he noted with satisfaction that his tent mates were still asleep. Pulling his boots on, he quietly stepped between the cots and slipped through the tent flap into the warm morning sunshine. The camp was deceptively quiet, the sign of disciplined soldiers. That surprised him, for there were probably more civilians than soldiers in Lorkan's army.

He was about to go look for something to eat, if there was still anything left over from breakfast, when a young man approached carrying a tray with a mug of ale and a plate of steaming eggs and sausage.

"Good morning, my Lord," the young man said with a smile. "It's not much, but I hope it meets with your satisfaction." He was a slender lad in his mid-teens, with curly blond hair and bright eyes like he was on some wonderful adventure.

Conal's mouth watered and his eyes lit up. "This looks excellent. Thank you." Accepting the tray, he glanced around for a place to sit.

"I'll go get you a chair, my Lord." He started to turn Conal stopped him.

"I'm fine. Thank you." He strode over to sit against a thick oak tree, crossing his legs and inhaled the aroma of hot food. This was far better fare than when he was with Oscon. Even the sleeping arrangements far exceeded anything Oscon ever found.

"Are you sure my Lord?"

"I'm positive. Thank you."

The young man dipped his head. "I am Bedo, my Lord. If you need anything, anything at all, I will get it for you."

"Thank you Bedo," Conal said with a chuckle. "I'm fine." The young man certainly had enthusiasm. When Bedo didn't wander off but simply stood to the side, Conal repeated, "I'm fine, Bedo. You can go about your work."

"I am, my Lord. I am your runner, your personal assistant, your servant." Bedo grinned like there was no better job in the world.

"You are?" Conal sipped the ale then sliced a bite of sausage. The ale was surprisingly good, especially here in the field.

"Yes, Lord Darr – uh… I mean, my Lord." Bedo swallowed hard at his faux pas.

Conal stopped mid-chew and pointed the knife at him, his eyes narrowing with an intense stare. "If I hear anyone calling me or even referring to me by that name, I will slice his throat and feed it to the ravens. My name is Conal, C-O-N-A-L. Got it?"

"Yes, my Lord," Bedo said in a rush. "I'm so sorry. I'll never do it again. I promise."

When Conal saw the fear in the man's eyes, he relaxed. "Apology accepted. Let's forget about it. Tell me Bedo, where do you hail from and how is it that you are here with Commander Lorkan?" He piled a portion of eggs on top of the bite of sausage.

"I am from just outside Havengarde, my Lord. I am here because King Torian murdered my family." The light briefly departed from his eyes.

Conal locked his gaze on him and softly intoned, "Just like he did mine... both of them."

Bedo frowned in puzzlement. "Both of them, my Lord?"

"Yes. First he murdered my father and mother and usurped the throne. Then he murdered the family who put their lives at risk to raise me in safety."

"So it's true," Bedo marveled. "You really are the king."

"Not yet," Conal replied with a smile. "But with the help of men like yourself and Lorkan and others, I hope to reclaim what is mine."

Lorkan walked up, looking refreshed and content. "Good morning, m'Lord. Sleep well?"

"Very," Conal said with a cheerful grin.

"Is Bedo taking good care of you?"

"Yes, thank you. He and I were just getting acquainted."

"He's a miller's son so he's not acquainted with the finer points of the role of a royal retainer. I'll search for someone more suitable as time goes on."

Out the corner of his eye, Conal saw Bedo put on a brave smile, though he was crestfallen. "Actually, I prefer we leave things as they are. Bedo strikes me as an intelligent young man and will fit the bill admirably. Besides, we have more important things to worry about than looking for retainers when we have one right here."

Bedo's disappointment morphed to hope that Conal's word outweighed Lorkan's.

"It will be as you wish, m'Lord." Lorkan smiled, pleased that Conal was not like so many other pompous asses of royalty whose disdain for the common man often revealed their own glaring shortcomings. "We did have an interesting incident during the evening, m'Lord."

"Yes?" Conal chewed the last bite and swigged down the last of the ale, handing off the tray to Bedo as he stood. "Thank you Bedo."

"You are welcome, my Lord Conal." Accepting the tray, he turned to go clean the plate and mug.

"You've made him very happy, m'Lord," Lorkan observed as Bedo strutted away.

"I like him. He's… um, enthusiastic."

Lorkan chuckled. "That he is. Like I said, he's a miller's son. His parents were murdered when they couldn't pay the increased poll tax. They were supposedly used as an example to all the others who had second thoughts about sequestering enough to feed themselves. We picked him up on the road to Rexfyrd. How he managed to get that far is anyone's guess. He's resourceful."

"You were saying about an incident," Conal reminded him.

"Yes." He motioned with his hands for Conal to follow him. "We captured four individuals trying to infiltrate our perimeter. They're not soldiers and they're not local. When questioned, they claimed they were dragon hunters." He abruptly stopped and tilted his head to give Conal a look of disbelief. "They claimed we had a dragon with us."

CHAPTER 17

Gwen

Gwen stood before a crescent-shaped stone table, where seven people were seated and stared at her. Marjorie sat in the center, with three men to her right and three women to her left. When Marjorie had told her that the Council wanted to see her, she had no idea how intimidating it would be.

Each of the members was middle-aged, with Marjorie clearly being the eldest. They all matched her, wearing the same silver trimmed blue robes. Gwen felt naked under their eyes like they could see into her mind and read her thoughts. It was foolish of her to feel that way, she knew, but she felt so vulnerable in their presence.

"Quinlee rí Túath," Marjorie said. "Welcome to the Council of Librarians. As you know, we are all wizards. Like all Prestiges, we seek knowledge and power. The Great Library is a vast source for all who would seek to learn and grow, regardless of their pursuits and race."

The other members at the table nodded and murmured their agreement.

"Yet, there is an encroaching darkness coming. King Torian thinks himself an emperor and is working towards invading every kingdom around him, including Steepcross. The rumors whispered are many, but we know for certain that Grimmar the Mage-Breaker is behind it all. He has corrupted Isentol, and we also

175

believe he ensorcelled Torian into killing his brother, the rightful king."

"I thought Grimmar hated magic and all those who practice it?" Gwen asked. She thought back to the man who'd entered the Chamber of the Altar. He was an agent of Grimmar and didn't look at all like a Prestige.

"So he says," Marjorie replied. "It is all a ruse. He has gained the allegiance of many Prestiges who want to control magic. We cannot allow that to happen. This Council has long held a position of neutrality in the world, but it cannot be so anymore."

The members at the table looked at Marjorie in surprise. The woman had obviously not shared that information before this meeting. Gwen was hoping these wizards would pledge their cause to the rebellion and join the fight against Torian. If what Marjorie said about Grimmar was true, they would need all the magical help they could muster.

"I see that you have two runes. Do you want more?"

"Yes." Gwen didn't even have to consider the question.

"Those of us before you have mastered something no other wizard has. What I am about to share with you cannot be repeated outside of this chamber. Do I have your word?"

"I won't say anything."

"Swear it," Marjorie said.

"I swear."

"Good. You know that only mages can bestow runes to other mages, yes?"

Gwen nodded slowly.

"Did you also know that mages can become so powerful that they ascend in power and become a wizard?"

"No, I did not. I'm still new to all of this."

"I can promise you that even the most seasoned Prestiges do not know this. It is something this council has discovered through many years of research. Once, we were all mages."

"What does that mean, exactly?" Gwen scrunched her brows in confusion.

"We are wizards, but we can bestow runes," Marjorie said plainly.

Gwen's face lit up in understanding.

"You know that the process of receiving a rune can be painful, so I will not caution you with fluffed words. These runes are powerful, most of them meant to be wielded as weapons in battle. As Simon can attest, this power comes with a burden."

Simon was the man next to her. He stood and pulled his robes open, revealing a crisscross of black lines across his chest. They pulsed visibly like unholy veins, the darkness standing in stark contrast to his pale skin.

"What is that?" Gwen asked.

"It is the residue of dark magic," Simon replied, closing his robes. "Few are brave enough to truly delve into its practice, and fewer still are strong enough to survive using it."

"You can choose which runes you want to take," Marjorie said. "I only want you to see the … consequences … that might arise."

When Gwen had first envisioned being covered in runes, she had found the idea appalling, fearing that she would be ugly. Then she met Aimil and decided that while she didn't want as many runes on her own body, they were not a blight upon her flesh as she thought. Gwen looked down at the runes on her hands.

Tintreach and *Saol.* Lightning and Life.

Gwen knew she would need all the power she could get. If her skin looked like Simon's in the end, then she hoped she could one day find someone who would love her despite the flaws to her skin. If she lived that long.

"I will accept them all," she said.

"Very well. Choose who your first rune will—"

A knock on the chamber door cut off the rest of her words. One of the women rose from her chair and hurried to the door. She opened it a few inches and shared a whispered conversation with one of the librarians, then returned to the table carrying a letter and passed it down to Marjorie. Gwen watched her open it and waited anxiously to continue with the runes.

"It seems a meeting has been called," Marjorie said. "The rebellion is requesting an emissary from the Great Library."

"Let us send one, then," Simon said. "As you said, we must cease being a neutral party."

"Does anyone object?" Marjorie asked.

None of the other members said anything.

"Once we complete our business with Quinlee, then we shall decide on who to send."

"Where is the meeting to be held?" Gwen asked, wishing that Marjorie would quit using that ridiculous name.

"Haddence," she replied. "It's on the border of Isentol and Clagmoran."

"When?" Gwen figured that would be the best place to report Aimil's crime, but she would need to get there in time.

"It's in two days. Now, for the matter of your runes. Please choose who you would like to receive a rune from first."

"Perhaps it would be best to start from one end of the table," Gwen motioned toward the women and swept her arm across, "and work down."

"A good suggestion," Marjorie said. "Sophia, if you would."

Sophia, the woman at the end of the left side of the table, stood and came around to join Gwen. She was slightly taller than Gwen with shoulder-length brown hair that was tied in a ponytail. Sophia stretched out her hand, directing it toward Gwen's forehead, and closed her eyes. Gwen closed hers as well and focused on the *bunús*. The magic flowing around Sophia and the others glowed brightly, except for Simon. An inky cloud surrounded him, pulsing and flickering with flashes of dark purple. It reminded Gwen of a storm cloud, only more sinister.

The rune Sophia offered hovered at the edge of Gwen's mind. It was wholesome and pure and felt similar to the *Saol* rune.

"*Leighis,*" Gwen said, speaking the rune's name.

An arc of white energy penetrated Gwen's body, weaving through the strands of her being and knitting itself into her. Gwen gasped as the pain flooded her, but just as quickly as it had come, it was gone.

"*Leighis* is a rune of healing." Sophia's voice broke the silence and Gwen opened her eyes.

The familiar pain of a new rune throbbed in her right hand and she lifted her arm to view it. Her flesh was raised and pink, and just above the *Saol* rune was her newest addition. It was a circle, surrounded by a square, surrounded by a triangle.

"If anyone is injured, you can use the *leighis* to heal them."

"Thank you," Gwen said, lowering her arm. Sophia returned to the table and the next woman came to take her place at Gwen's side. This woman was shorter than Gwen by a foot, but her red hair, green eyes, and fiery expression spoke volumes about her fierceness.

"I am Tala," she said. "Lift yer hand and open yer palm."

Gwen did as Tala asked, but the woman shook her head. "No, do not show me your palm. *Open* it."

"I don't understand," Gwen said.

Tala's green eyes twinkled mischievously and she drew a dagger from within her robes and handed it to Gwen. Realization dawned on Gwen and she hesitantly accepted the blade. She glanced at Marjorie, concerned something was amiss, but the elderly woman nodded, a comforting smile tugging at her lips. Gwen pressed the tip of the dagger to her palm. She swallowed her fear and pressed down slightly. The blade was sharp and easily cut into her flesh.

"That will do," Tala said. She took the dagger back and wiped the blood on Gwen's shirt, then cut her own palm with the blade. Tala held her hand over Gwen's to align their cuts, then whispered something under her breath.

Gwen's palm tingled, lightly at first, then it grew in intensity until her skin grew uncomfortably warm.

"Speak the rune," Tala said, though her eyes were still closed.

Gwen felt for the *bunús* rune and connected her mind to it. She was startled to see roaring flames spinning around Tala's hand, but she quickly understood what the rune's power was.

"*Tine,*" Gwen said its name.

The flames from Tala's hand coursed into her, searing through the cut in her palm. Gwen's entire body grew hot and she could feel droplets of sweat slide down her face. With a whooshing sound, the flames died and her body's temperature returned to normal.

"Fire," Gwen rasped, her throat parched.

"Aye, fire. It's as wild and untamed as anything ye'll ever come across."

Gwen had only taken two runes, but her legs were starting to tremor and she was feeling lightheaded. She felt the fire rune on her left side, just under her armpit. The sensitive skin ached with pain.

"Do you need to rest?" Marjorie asked. "You don't look so good."

"I think I can do another," Gwen said, stubbornly trying to force her legs to quit shaking.

Marjorie looked to the next woman. "Beloria."

Beloria bowed her head to Marjorie. She didn't leave the table but instead stared intently at Gwen. She said nothing and hardly moved. Gwen grew troubled under her gaze, but she matched Beloria's stare and tried not to blink. Something at the edge of her vision floated toward her, but when Gwen tried to focus on it, it faded from view.

"Focus," Beloria said. "Focus on the *bunús*."

Gwen knew that the *bunús* was the key to unlocking the power of the runes, but each time she channeled into it, she felt herself grow weaker. She drew a deep breath and closed her eyes. The *bunús* rune was there in her mind and she mentally reached for it. The magic funneled in and out of her, igniting her runes but stealing her strength.

One more and I can rest for a moment, she told herself.

The floating thing she saw before was a rune. Now that she was connected to the *bunús,* she saw it clearly. It came toward her, guided by an unseen force, and landed on her chest.

"*Láidreacht,*" Gwen said.

The rune rested where her heart was and after she spoke its name, it fused to her skin. The power of the rune took the rest of her strength, but it also gave her some in exchange. The vigor it offered was different than what it took, but it was a reciprocal action and Gwen felt the tremor in her legs fade.

"This rune feels weird," Gwen said. "Weird, but ..." she struggled for the right word, clenching her hand into a fist.

"Strong?" Beloria asked.

"Yes," Gwen replied excitedly.

"The rune grants might. When you tap into it, you'll find yourself capable of feats you never imagined."

Gwen channeled the rune and spoke its name. Her muscles flooded with renewed energy. The weakness she felt before was completely gone.

"I can do another rune," she said confidently.

"Are you sure?" Marjorie asked. "It would not be wise to push yourself too hard."

"I'm fine," Gwen replied. "I feel like I could do this all day."

Marjorie frowned at her, but she acquiesced. The old woman left her spot at the table and came to kneel in front of Gwen.

"This rune will leave two marks," she said. "One on each of your legs. It will require twice the energy, so you must be mindful when you use it."

"I understand."

Once again, Gwen closed her eyes and went through the process of linking her mind to the *bunús*. A ghostly falcon took shape and circled the room. It dived down, splitting into two, and each bird struck her outer thighs. Gwen's knees buckled and she dropped, cracking her kneecaps roughly against the stone floor. She could feel the runes searing her skin, but the flow of magic wasn't opening up. Gwen struggled against the burning pain, trying to focus on the name of the rune. It eluded her for a brief moment, but it was long enough that she started to panic.

"*Luas!*" she finally cried out. Her thoughts blurred and darkness claimed her.

When Gwen opened her eyes, her face was touching the cold floor. She forced herself onto her knees and then heaved herself to her feet. Marjorie stood nearby, a look of concern on her face.

"I warned you about pushing yourself," she said.

"I know," Gwen replied, rubbing the side of her face. "It just took me by surprise. I'm fine, I promise."

"I think we should take a break. Sophia, can you get Quinlee something to drink?"

Gwen was secretly glad that Marjorie called for a break. She didn't want to appear weak or unworthy of their runes, and it made her feel better that she wasn't the one temporarily giving in. She accepted a wooden cup from Sophia and drank its contents, expecting water and getting a taste of wine instead. Gwen coughed and cleared her throat, then drank the rest of it and wiped her chin on her sleeve.

"Please call me Gwen. It's the name I've known all my life."

"As long as you are in my domain, you will suffer my will. Quinlee is your true name and it is the one I will use."

Gwen rolled her eyes when Marjorie wasn't looking. She gently rubbed at the fire rune on her side. Of all the ones she'd received so far, it was the most painful.

"Is the girl ready?" Simon asked. "I have many things that require my attention."

"Patience is a virtue," Marjorie said to him.

"And it's one that I lack," Simon replied, scowling.

Marjorie looked at Gwen. "Do you need more time to rest? We can continue later if needed."

Gwen shook her head. As much as she wanted to rest, she knew that time was running short if she was going to get Aimil to Haddence in time for the meeting.

"Don't be a fool," Marjorie lowered her voice. "Simon's rune can kill you if you aren't careful."

"I can do this," Gwen said, casting a glance at Simon. He drummed his fingers on the stone table impatiently.

"Very well. I warned you. If you die, my hands are clean." Marjorie returned to the table.

"My lord Simon," Gwen said, raising her voice. "I'm ready."

"Call me librarian," Simon replied, rising from the table. Gwen thought him the most intimidating. His head was shaved and his scalp glistened with a thin layer of sweat. As he drew near, Gwen saw there were black lines around his blue irises. They resembled the ones on his chest and Gwen found them alluring in their own way.

"Power can be born from fear," Simon said, then grabbed Gwen by her throat.

She tried to break away from his grasp, but he was stronger than her. He clenched his fingers tighter, constricting her flow of air and she began to panic. Gwen clawed at his hands, raking his flesh with her nails. Simon was unfazed. He backed her against the wall and Gwen looked to the other members for help. They sat quietly, watching. Gwen didn't understand. He was trying to kill her and they were doing nothing!

It was a trap.

Gwen's thoughts became a confusing swirl. It was because she was Kamron's daughter. Someone else had found out about her identity and threatened their power if they didn't do something about her. Or was Aimil behind this? Did she know about the vial?

Use your runes. It was Marjorie's voice in her head. *Simon's magic is dark. It requires a darker means of transfer.*

Trying to kill someone was a way of sharing a rune? Gwen wasn't so sure she wanted that type of magic now, but it was too late to change her mind. She summoned the power of the strength rune and choked out its name.

"*Láidreacht.*"

The magic flowed through her body and she grabbed ahold of Simon's wrist. She squeezed hard and felt something crunch. Still, Simon didn't let go, but his grip weakened enough for Gwen to force his hand off her throat. She gasped in a deep breath and balled her hand into a fist, striking Simon directly in the chest.

He staggered back and his robes fell open, revealing the dark lines on his chest. One of the lines had been damaged by her punch and the inky darkness dripped down his skin. It coalesced at his naval and then sprang into the air, splattering across her forehead. Gwen screamed though it was more in surprise than pain. The liquid dripped down into her eyes, blinding her. She tried to rub it away to no avail.

Gwen saw the rune in the darkness. It was twisted and jagged and looked nothing like the others. The rune reminded her of a thorn bush. There was nothing beautiful about it. It was nothing but pain and anger and death. Yet, she spoke its name anyway.

"*Draein saoil.*"

Her vision slowly returned, but it wasn't the same as before. There was a murkiness to everything as if she were looking at the world through a dark lense.

"No more," Gwen begged. "No more runes."

CHAPTER 18

Conal

"A dragon?" Conal snorted a laugh. "You hiding something I should know about?"

Lorkan grinned in response. "I know. Still, I do find it odd that they were so intent to come into my camp."

"I assume you've interrogated them beyond the fact that they're dragon hunters."

"We've done a quick assessment and other than them saying they're dragon hunters, we can't get much out of them. They're strange." Lorkan pointed across the open field dotted with small individual wedge tents to four individuals, their hands tied behind them, sitting on the ground around a fire pit whose embers had long since cooled. Two guards kept careful watch over them.

"In what way?"

"It's hard to describe, m'Lord. I thought it best for you to see for yourself."

As Conal and Lorkan approached, the four captives jerked their heads around to gape up at them. Three of the captives were women, young attractive women like the woman Conal saw during his visit with Krag. They all had the wild look of a cornered hare, yet their eyes had the glassy glaze of drug induced stupor.

Conal pointed to a woman about his age, strawberry blond hair folding over a smooth face with blue eyes and a pert nose. Except for the almost rabid look in her eyes, she was very pretty.

"Stand that one up," he commanded.

She yelped as one guard yanked her to standing.

Conal walked behind her to gaze down at her hands. Reaching down, he gently twisted her bound hand to reveal the tattoo of a dragon's head with a lance through it. With a frustrated sigh, he turned to Lorkan. "You'll get nothing from them. They are what they say they are. Why they are here is odd." In truth, Conal knew it had it had something to do with Bryok and he wondered if Bryok's rune was glowing.

"Why do they all have that strange look?" Lorkan asked.

Conal ticked his head at him to come over. "See that?" He pointed to the tattoo. "They've all been rune-marked."

"What does that mean?"

"It means that someone believes that dragons are still around. This person is also a rune-master. He or she put these brands on these dragon hunters. What it does is bind them to the rune-master. No, it's not what you think," he said when he saw the fear in Lorkan's eyes. "These people wanted to do this, but it was all based upon a lie. They were promised untold riches for finding and killing a dragon. They were told stories of unimagined wealth, living the idle life of never having to work again, of having servants and slaves at your beck and call."

"But look at them," Lorkan said. "They look like they've been drugged. How can they expect to find and kill a dragon in that condition... providing a dragon even exists?"

"They believe it does and the rune-master behind them also believes it. They will persist until they either find a dragon and kill it or die in the process. The question is, what do we do with them? We can't allow them to hinder or compromise our operation."

The woman's stupor abruptly vanished, and she quivered with excitement. A burst of murmuring erupted from the three on the ground. Conal looked up to see Bryok approaching, his face tight.

The woman stared at him with glee. "Dragon."

Lorkan cocked an eyebrow and exchanged a look with Conal. "They're crazy."

"I know," Conal readily agreed, noting the low glow of the rune on Bryok's arm.

"What do we have here?" Bryok asked, doing his best to appear ignorant.

"Dragon hunters," Lorkan replied. "And apparently they think you're a dragon."

Bryok frowned at Lorkan then splayed his arms and slowly bent his head to look at his own body, his head twisting side to side. In a deliberate gesture, he looked behind him. "I don't have a tail or wings. Does that mean I can't fly? How disappointing."

"Can you breathe fire?" Conal asked with exaggerated hope.

Bryok loudly exhaled and shook his head. "No. Just morning breath, which some have accused as smelling like dragon's breath, which never made any sense to me because it would imply they'd actually smelled a dragon's breath." He fluttered a hand in front of his mouth.

Lorkan smirked.

"Dragon," the woman repeated, taking a step towards Bryok and struggling to free her hands.

The other three jerked and twisted, trying to stand only to be held down by the guards whose threats did not stop their struggling. Yet the sole focus of the dragon hunters was on Bryok.

Conal realized that as long as Bryok stayed with them, the dragon hunters would be a problem, a big problem.

"This is all rather strange," Lorkan observed, staring at Bryok. "They didn't show up until you showed up."

"It's happened before," Conal explained.

"It has?"

"On the way to Denhelm. We had four of them come out of the woods hot in pursuit of Bryok."

Lorkan cast a suspicious eye on Bryok. "Why?"

"I am a druid, remember?" Bryok parried. "You'd be surprised at the number of lunatics I get chasing after me once they find out I'm a druid, everything from wanting their fortunes told to making it rain on their farm while denying rain to the neighbor they don't like."

"But why dragon hunters and why now?"

Bryok fixed him with a sharp gaze. "Torian seeks to rule over all the kingdoms and will leave nothing to chance. It is obvious that he believes dragons exist and has sent out these poor fools to find them. The problem is that anyone or anything magical attracts them like bees to a pollinating flower. I'm only a druid. Can you imagine what it must be like to be a mage or wizard and have to fend these creatures off?"

"You're a druid," Lorkan said. "Can't you do something to fix it?

"Were it that easy," Bryok replied rolling his eyes. "You see that tattoo? It's a rune-mark. If you examine it closely, you'll see the runes. But more importantly, once you are rune-marked, you can never go back." He slid a meaningful glance at Conal. "In their case, they are forever marked as dragon hunters."

"What should we do with them?"

"Do you want them following you and continuing to advertise where you are?"

Lorkan turned to Conal. "We can't have them following us, m'Lord. Torian has already sent warring parties across the borders of Tir Manach. Caldyr does nothing to stop him. Were it not for Commander Sorcha, Torian would be at the sea by now."

"Who is Sorcha?" Conal asked.

"She's a former regimental commander. She spoke out against Caldyr's submission to Torian and barely escaped with her life. However, she was much loved and before Caldyr realized it, a third of his army had deserted. Her operations are to our north in Brody's demesne."

"Caldyr allows this?" Bryok said, an eyebrow raised.

"Caldyr has sent urgent demands for troops," Lorkan answered, frowning at the dragon hunters who were staring at Bryok with uncontained fascination. "We intercepted two messages meant for Pharyl."

"And Pharyl doesn't know all this is going on?" Conal knitted his brow, wondering if he had missed the signals while he was in Hemlyn.

"I can't say, m'Lord," Lorkan replied. "What I can say is that I wouldn't trust him."

Conal swiveled his head to stare at Bryok. "He knows who I am. It's just a matter of time before he directs his attention here."

"We assumed that, m'Lord," Lorkan interrupted. "That's why we intercepted you on the way to Caldyr."

"Where's Drustan?" Bryok interjected.

"He's still with Voldar and the dwarf forces near the four corners where the kingdoms meet. That is where we are headed."

"Then you have a plan in place?" Conal asked, hoping someone smarter than he had thought this all out.

"Not completely, m'Lord," admitted. "We head down to connect with King Rorkyn. We're praying that the forces to the east have likewise mobilized."

"What do we know about them?"

"Not much, m'Lord. Drustan probably knows more."

"What about Sorcha –"

"We don't have time to chase her down," Bryok asserted. "We know we can depend on the forces she has. It's merely a question of coordinating the attack. We need to get south to Clagmoran and find out if Kilmaryn is with us. We're wasting time."

"What do we do with them?" Lorkan ticked his head at the dragon hunters.

"Kill them," Bryok flatly stated.

Lorkan's jaw tightened. "We're not murderers."

"Then give me a better solution," Bryok retorted.

"They're here because of you," Lorkan countered.

"And if Drustan were here, we'd have the same problem," Conal pointed out.

"Or any other person with magic powers," Bryok added then narrowed his gaze at Lorkan. "Will you have magic with you when you attack Torian? Because if you don't, even the gods can't help you."

"We are not murderers," Lorkan stubbornly insisted.

"Is it because you disarmed them?" Bryok challenged. "Then give them back their weapons and I will fight them. I will do what you are unwilling to do."

"What's all the fuss?" Torgreth called out, walking over to where Conal, Bryok, and Lorkan seemed to be in an argument. Galadyr strolled beside him, casually taking in the encampment.

"They captured four dragon hunters trying to infiltrate their lines," Conal answered, "and we're deciding what to do with them."

"What is to decide?" Galadyr calmly answered. "They are rune-bound to the mage master who serves Torian. If you believe Torian to be good, then release them. If Torian is evil, then those who willingly serve him are likewise evil. When you defeat Torian, will you set him free?"

Lorkan immediately understood, but the sour expression on his face said he still didn't like it. "Is it your wish, m'Lord?"

"Trying to absolve yourself?" Bryok tartly said.

"Everyone just stop," Conal commanded. "Arguing like this gets us nowhere. I'll do it." He started to unsheathe his sword when a voice stopped him.

"I'll take care of it, Boss," Maldwic boldly said, striding up, Seren and two others walking with him.

Conal slid his sword back in the sheath, both pleased and impressed with the man. "Thank you, Commander."

"You all go about your affairs," Maldwic said, "while we take care of business at hand."

Immediately feeling like his authority had been usurped, Lorkan held a hand up, exhaling a long-suffering sigh. "Thank you, Commander, but this is my responsibility. I'm the one who allowed them into my camp. I will deal with it."

Maldwic looked at Conal. "Boss?"

"He's right. It *is* his responsibility." Without waiting for a comment, he headed back to his tent where Bedo waited for him.

Maldwic hustled to catch up to him and matching strides as they walked. "Got some info for you, Boss. Overheard Lorkan's scouts reporting a large force crossed the border into Tir Manach and heading south."

Assuming Lorkan didn't know yet, Conal jerked to a halt and spun around to see the four captives kneeling and lined up in a row, Lorkan and three others standing behind them. Bryok stood two paces away in front of the captives, Torgreth and Galadyr behind him. With their attention devoted to Bryok, the captives didn't see or notice when Lorkan gave the command. In one uniform motion, he and the others raised their swords and in a fierce arc, sliced through the necks, separating heads from quivering bodies.

The deed done, Lorkan stood surveying the scene, reconciling distaste with necessity. Two women soldiers approached him.

"Those are the scouts," Maldwic revealed.

Though Conal couldn't hear what was said, he saw Lorkan straighten, question the two scouts then make a beeline towards him.

"M'Lord. Enemy troops about an hour away, heading south. We need to intercept them."

"Take charge. We'll follow your lead."

"Thank you, m'Lord. We leave in ten minutes."

Two hours of hard riding gave Lorkan's army time to set up an ambush. His scouts estimated the enemy strength at around 500, moving in cohort units of 50, each cohort led by a junior officer. The enemy commander, a large man with a perpetual scowl, sat upon a large steed, controlling his forces from the middle. Lorkan was impressed for the man moved his army as one with experience. Yet that mattered little for Lorkan's army outnumbered his opponent by 6:1.

Lorkan arranged his ambush in box pattern with the lid open, allowing the enemy to enter the box before Lorkan closed it with a rear guard. Much to Lorkan's distress, Conal refused to stay out of harm's way, firmly informing him that he intended to fully participate, positioning himself with Maldwic's small force blocking the road.

Lorkan had chosen the terrain well for the road the enemy followed undulated along the side of a mountain in a series of curves that blocked what was in front or behind. All they had to do now was wait.

"Never been in a real battle," Torgreth offhandedly commented, a double-bladed axe in his hand. "But I do know how to handle an ax."

"I am sure you will excel, my friend," Galadyr reassured him. The elf had chosen a longbow along with half a dozen quivers stuffed with arrows. Together, he and the dwarf stood inside the tree line beside the road where it sharply curved as it bent back on itself. Conal and Bryok stood opposite them across the road. Maldwic's small force, along with 300 of Lorkan's army filled in behind them.

Just as the enemy's lead scouts rounded the corner a ram's horn sounded and the shouts of battle filled the air.

Conal raced forward, easily outdistancing his friends and hurled himself past the scouts who had fallen, pierced with arrows from Galadyr's perfect aim. In short order, Conal came upon the main body already in the melee of battle as Lorkan's forces attacked from both sides. Trusting the power of his runes, Conal dove headlong into the fight, a crazed dervish destroying everything in his path.

All too quickly, the enemy gave ground, pressed hard from the sides, but especially from the vehemence of Conal's attack for he had cut a path through the enemy as he forged his way to the commander who by now realized that his position was lost.

In a vain attempt to rally his troops, the commander called for retreat only to find his escape route was blocked. Accepting fate that he and his army were lost, the commander dismounted and slapped the horse on the rear, sending him away then turned to do battle, surprised that he suddenly faced a man smaller than he, who had managed to carve his way here, the strewn bodies of the dead behind him.

"Who are you?"

Conal's eyes blazed and he felt a sudden surge of overwhelming strength as he answered, "I am Conal, the son of the true king of Isentol."

"That king is dead," the commander retorted.

"Just as you will be."

The commander raised his sword to block Conal's attack, immediately feeling as though a granite anvil had crashed into him. He felt a tingling in his arm as it weakened. Yet he hadn't counted on Conal's speed for no sooner had the downward stroke smashed into him, he felt a sharp pain and a sudden warmth across his stomach. He looked down to see his stomach sliced open. He raised his head just in time to see his last vision while still alive, a vision of a man whose cold angry eyes spoke of revenge before the world went black.

Once the commander went down, the enemy's will to fight withered and died. Throwing down swords and axes and bows, they stood in place and surrendered.

His berserker's rage draining away, Conal inhaled a deep breath, surveying the bloody battlefield of broken bodies and the cries of the mortally wounded. Movement out the corner of his eye caught his attention and he twisted his head in time to see Bryok lurching into the forest, an arrow through his chest.

CHAPTER 19

Gwen

Gwen sat alone in Marjorie's personal chamber, nursing her pained flesh and bruised throat. Her experience with Simon had been violent and unexpected. Again, she lamented accepting the rune before knowing fully what it would require to accept it—and what it would cost her.

The door to the chamber creaked open and Gwen jumped involuntarily.

"I told her she needs to rest, but she refuses to," Marjorie was saying to Aimil as they walked into the room.

Gwen stood up and clenched her jaw to keep her teeth from chattering. Simon's rune was making her body thrum with power. And she was burning up, her flesh hot to the touch.

"We need to get on the road," Gwen said.

"We can leave tomorrow," Aimil replied, frowning at her. "You look like the gods stole your soul."

"I feel like they did," Gwen replied. The fingers of her right hand started tremoring and she balled them into a fist, her nails digging into her palm and reopening her cut. She didn't even feel the pain, barely felt the blood slicking between her fingers.

"Are you all right?" Aimil asked. She stepped closer, looking Gwen up and down. When their gazes locked, Aimil's eyes widened briefly, but it was long enough that Gwen saw the surprise in them. And possibly fear.

"You took a dark rune?" Her tone was on the border of incredulous.

"I didn't know," Gwen muttered.

"No one warned her?" Aimil asked, turning to Marjorie.

"I tried to, but she was adamant in her decision. Simon even showed her his lines."

Aimil made a noise in her throat, clearly displeased. She shook her head and grabbed Gwen by the hand and led her out of the room.

"Where are you going?" Marjorie asked, following after them.

"We're leaving," Aimil said. "And you can't stop us."

"I won't stop you. You are free to come and go as you choose. Gwen said she wanted all of the runes we offered, and I want to make certain she's changed her mind."

"I'm certain," Gwen said. "Thank you for everything, but we need to reach Haddence and we're already short on time."

"Very well," Marjorie said. "Farewell Quinlee. May we meet again."

Gwen offered a tired smile before Aimil continued pulling her down the hall. All Gwen wanted to do was sleep, but she knew she didn't have time to rest. Not yet. Aimil led her through the library and then suddenly they were back at the stable. Gwen looked around, confused as to how they got there. She had no recollection of anything other than being in the library.

"How did we get here?" she asked.

Aimil gave her an odd look. "We walked," she said.

"The whole way?"

"You need to sleep," Aimil said.

"I can't. We have to get to Haddence."

"Why? What's in Haddence?"

Gwen's jaw quivered against her will and she waited for it to subside before answering. "The leaders of the rebellion are holding a meeting. It's in two d-days," she stammered.

"Even if you were rested, we couldn't make that trip in two days."

"We have to try," Gwen said pleadingly. "We *have* to."

Aimil shrugged. "Fine. It's your funeral."

No, it'll be yours, Gwen thought.

The stable boy brought their horses out and Gwen struggled to climb into the saddle. Her muscles were like jelly. With the help of the boy and Aimil, she was able to get situated and Aimil led the way out of the city, following the wall until they reached the main gates, then taking the road northwest.

Gwen weaved in and out of consciousness, her eyes refusing to stay open. She swayed in the saddle and almost fell off her horse several times before she leaned forward and laid her head against the horse's neck and succumbed to her exhaustion. When she came to, they were still riding, and the city behind them was long gone.

"I thought you died," Aimil said from beside her. "I had to check your pulse to be sure."

"How long was I out?"

"About an hour."

Gwen was surprised to hear that. She felt like she'd been asleep for days. Despite the shortness of her nap, she felt invigorated. The strength had returned to her muscles and the tremors were gone. Her body still thrummed with magic from the dark rune, but her body temperature was back to normal.

"I can't believe you took a dark rune," Aimil said. "Most mages don't survive the process."

"It was pretty sadistic," Gwen confessed. "I thought Simon was going to choke the life out of me."

They rode in silence for a short time, then Aimil asked, "Who gave you the runes?"

Gwen opened her mouth to reply, then caught herself. Marjorie had sworn her to secrecy regarding the Council's ability to bestow runes despite the fact they were wizards, and she didn't want their wrath coming down on her.

"The council members had some of their assistant mages give me runes," Gwen lied. She could feel Aimil's gaze on her and suspected the woman knew she was lying.

"Simon is one of the assistant mages?"

"Yes."

"Interesting. That's also the name of one of the council members," Aimil said casually.

"And?"

"You're hiding something," Aimil accused.

"It's funny that you should think that," Gwen replied. "Considering I know what *you* did."

"I've done many things. You'll have to be more specific."

"Just forget it," Gwen huffed. She wasn't in the mood for this, nor did she want to confront Aimil yet. She wanted the rebellion leaders present when she laid out the events of Auleavell.

"Are you afraid you'll upset me?" Aimil laughed. "Spit it out already."

Gwen ignored her until Aimil brought her horse closer and grabbed ahold of her wrist. "What is it you want to say?" Aimil asked. Her tone was serious, menacing almost.

"Let go of me," Gwen demanded, trying to jerk free of Aimil's grasp. When Aimil didn't release her, Gwen got angry. Her face flushed with heat and she looked Aimil in the eyes.

"I know you're the one who poisoned the Thaestra River."

Aimil's expression barely changed, but she stiffened slightly.

"What are you talking about?"

"You dropped the vial that held the poison," Gwen said. "I saw it. And Marjorie confirmed it was a magical poison."

"You told Marjorie it was mine?"

"No."

They stared at each other as the horses continued to trot along the road. Gwen's heart was racing in her chest. She was afraid. Aimil wasn't one to be trifled with.

"Why did you do it?"

Aimil shrugged. "Just following orders."

"What? Eradore told you to poison the river?" Gwen's mind couldn't fathom that.

"Of course not. Eradore is weak."

"Then who?" Gwen asked.

"I suppose there's no use in lying now that you know," Aimil said. "The order came from Torian."

Gwen almost fell off her horse in shock. "You … you're working for that tyrant?"

"Your surprise is cute. I told you before that I work for the highest bidder. Who do you think has more money? The rebellion? Don't be ridiculous."

Aimil was a traitor. She'd just admitted it. Gwen knew she was in trouble now. There was no way Aimil was going to let her continue living after revealing that. Gwen swallowed hard, her eyes going from Aimil to the road ahead. There was nothing but fields around them. Aimil would kill her and get away with it. Gwen snapped the reigns and her horse sped forward.

"You can't run!" Aimil shouted after her.

"Yah!" Gwen cried, urging her mount faster but the horse shrieked and staggered, its legs buckling. The animal collapsed, tipping to the side. Gwen threw herself from the saddle at the last moment, hitting the ground and rolling out of range. She got back onto her feet and saw the horse was dead. Blood seeped from its eyes and nostrils. Gwen turned to face Aimil as she approached. The woman was insane. She needed to be stopped, but Gwen had a fraction of the runes Aimil did. The odds were against her.

Three globes of green light appeared in Aimil's hand and she hurled them at Gwen. They struck the ground around her and the dirt and grass sizzled and melted. Gwen summoned the power of her fire rune and stretched out her arms, hoping the blast didn't harm the horse. She spoke the rune's name and released the magic. A wave of crackling fire poured from her palms. The rune on her side grew warm and tingled her skin.

Aimil cursed and spoke the name of a rune, erecting a magical shield around her and the horse. Gwen's flames struck the shield and fizzled out of existence. Aimil's mount came right at her, forcing Gwen to cut off the magic as she jumped over her fallen horse to get out of the way. Gwen was thrown to the ground as something heavy struck her from behind. Rough hands rolled her over and she looked up at Aimil. Had she jumped off her horse?

"What were you planning to do? Turn me over to Eradore?" Aimil punched her in the mouth and Gwen could feel warm blood on her lips. She licked it off and winced as her tongue touched the wound.

"Yes," Gwen replied. "You will pay for your crime."

Aimil laughed and punched her again. "I thought you had potential, but I was wrong. You're like the rest of them. Weak and foolish."

"Because I want freedom from oppression?"

"No, because you want to upset the order of things. If Torian wasn't meant to be king, Kamron would have fended him off and defeated his brother. Things always work out as they are intended to."

"You're insane," Gwen growled. She tried to buck Aimil off her but failed. Aimil punched her again and Gwen's vision blurred for a brief moment. She grabbed onto Aimil's wrists and tried to gain control. Gwen knew she wasn't as strong as Aimil, so she reached for the power of the might rune. Before she could summon its magic, the dark rune called out to her. Gwen flinched away mentally from the darkness, but its pull was undeniable.

"*Draein saoil,*" she uttered.

The magic flared to life and Gwen felt an influx of energy entering her body. She didn't understand what was happening at first. Aimil gasped and tried to break away from her, but the rune held her firmly in place. And then Gwen realized what the rune's power was.

It was sucking the lifeforce out of Aimil. Gwen's stomach churned and she felt sick at the realization, but the rune continued to pull Aimil's energy away and filter it into Gwen. She wanted it to stop, yet she also wanted *more.* Her desires conflicted within her, a confusing whirl of dread and hunger.

"Stop," Aimil begged breathlessly. Her shoulders sagged and the life in her eyes grew dim. "Please."

Gwen wanted to stop, but she couldn't. The rune was directing her, bidding her to finish the task. "I ... can't," Gwen panted.

A shadow passed overhead, but Gwen was too focused on the thrilling feeling of Aimil's life being sucked away to care what it was until something roared and broke her focus, cutting off the magic. Aimil slumped backward and Gwen crawled out from under her, looking around fearfully.

The shadow passed over her again and Gwen looked up to see a massive silver dragon. It spiraled lower and lower until it landed, stirring up dust and loose grass. Gwen immediately recognized Venia from Auleavell.

"What are you doing here?" Gwen asked.

"Saving your life," Venia huffed. "Foolish humans!"

"I had it under control," Gwen replied.

"Is that why you almost killed her? Dark magic should never be used so carelessly. If you had taken her entire lifeforce into you, it would have killed both of you."

Gwen's expression turned horrified. "I wasn't ... how did you know what was happening?"

"Dragons see everything," Venia said.

Gwen remembered Venia saying that before, but she just assumed it was a figure of speech and not something literal.

"This isn't over," Aimil rasped.

Gwen looked at her in time to see a rune on her arm glow before she vanished.

"Where did she go?" Gwen demanded.

"Wherever she wanted, I suppose. That doesn't matter. Climb on my back."

"Do what?" Gwen asked.

"Get on my back. We're going to Haddence."

Gwen stared at Venia for a moment, thinking the dragon was joking, but Venia lowered her shoulder and waited patiently. Gwen slowly stepped closer and placed her hands on Venia's scales. She hesitated.

"We don't have all day," Venia growled.

Gwen climbed onto Venia's back and settled herself in a spot between the dragon's shoulders and neck. With a powerful flap of her wings, Venia launched into the air and Gwen screamed. Venia flew up, up, up, high into the air, then leveled out and headed northwest.

"Whatever you do, don't fall!" Venia roared into the air.

Gwen held on as tightly as she could and lowered her head against the wind. Aimil had betrayed her and the rebellion. She would tell Eradore everything.

And then she would track Aimil down and kill her.

CHAPTER 20

Conal

Conal leaped across dead bodies to chase after Bryok.

Torgreth saw him race away. "Where you going?"

"I'll be back," Conal shouted over his shoulder, plunging into the forest. Up ahead, he saw the struggling Bryok weaving unsteadily up the mountain. "Stop. What are you doing?"

Ignoring him, Bryok pressed on, staggering doggedly forward.

"Stop. Where are you going? You need help." Conal dodged trees to catch up, surprised that the mortally wounded man could maintain such a pace. Conal's speed kicked in and he managed to overtake the druid as he struggled over a rock cropping.

"Help me," Bryok gasped, lifting a weak hand to point higher up to what appeared to be a cave opening.

"Where are you going?" Conal grabbed Bryok's arm and placed it over his shoulder, wrapping the other arm around the druid's waist to help him walk.

"Up there."

"Why?"

"I'm dying."

"What's up there?" Conal's face hardened, a sudden feeling of overwhelming loss flooding within him.

"Safe…" Bryok's breathing became labored.

By now Bryok's legs straggled with each step and by the time they reached the cave, his legs dragged behind him, the toes of his boots leaving parallel trails on the leaf cluttered forest floor. Inside the cave, Conal gently placed Bryok on his side on the dirt floor and kneeled beside him. The arrow had penetrated close to the heart and the barbed end protruded out his back. With each heartbeat, blood pulsed out of the wound.

Conal glanced around the darkness, wondering how Bryok knew a cave was here. It was larger than he realized with a tall ceiling and going back for some distance.

Bryok's eyes fluttered as he struggled for breath. "Listen… not much time…"

"Yes?"

"Dragons… will help… you… must return…" He inhaled a rattling breath. "Give it back."

"Give what back?"

"Haven… Havengarde… dragons' home. Give it back. Sacred." Bryok groaned. "Few left… promise me…"

"Sure, I promise. What, what?"

"Protect us." Bryok's eyes closed.

"Protect who?" Conal pleaded.

Bryok opened his eyes to gaze at Conal. "Dragons. Only twelve left…. Eleven now. You must save us."

"I will; I promise." Though not understanding, Conal was willing to agree to anything.

Peace settled across Bryok's face and he smiled. "You are the one... I knew it... from the beginning." He closed his eyes and the tenseness in his body sloughed away.

Conal sat back, inhaling a mournful breath, feeling very much alone.

A dull silver glow enveloped Bryok's body and the rune on his arm began to glow, brighter and brighter. Suddenly the body began to stretch and grow, changing color and texture as it pushed out. Startled, Conal scooted back on hands and feet like a scuttling crab, watching as the body grew larger and larger, forming wings and a tail and the head of a dragon. The arrow, once protruding out Bryok's back, popped inside the dragon's chest though leaving a bloody wound behind, yet the feathered shaft remained visible near the dragon's heart.

Once the body stopped growing, Conal stood a gaped at the dead dragon stretched before him, his mind jumbled trying to comprehend what had just happened. Yet the all too obvious conclusion that Bryok was a dragon in human form was more than he could fathom. How was it possible?

Understanding began pushing its way through the overlapping and conflicting thoughts as the slavish pursuit by dragon hunters suddenly made sense. He startled as he suddenly realized that Drustan must also be a dragon in human form. Alarm vibrated within as Bryok's last words replayed.

"Dragons. Only twelve left.... Eleven now. You must save us."

His first instinct was to race back and urge Lorkan and the others to immediately head for Clagmoran or wherever Drustan was. But he remained and stared at the dragon who was once Bryok… or was this Krag? He shook his head realizing the real reason Bryok wasn't there when Krag came to visit.

What did he mean by 'give it back?'

Conal frowned as he stared at Krag, wondering what he should feel. He had come to like and depend on Bryok and at first had been upset at the man's passing. Yet that Bryok was a dragon knocked that emotion off the pedestal. Sure, he was upset, but… the man was a dragon. Should he be more upset, especially as there were only eleven dragons left.

He needed to get to Drustan before anything else happened.

Conal turned and stepped to the edge of the cave, realizing for the first time how high up it was as he stood on the edge and gazed out over the tops of the trees of the vast forest. Casting a last look back, he descended into the forest, wondering what Drustan was going to do or say once he found out his brother was dead.

His return elicited more than a few polite, yet stern, rebukes.

"Don't ever do that again," Galadyr quietly chastised. "While you are a formidable warrior, you are not impervious to injury or capture. You need to let us know where you are."

Conal wanted to say that he could take care of himself, but instead said, "You are right. My apologies. Bryok is dead."

213

"I know."

"You do?"

"I was too late to stop the archer who slew him."

Conal peered at him, recognizing the pain of guilt. "It's not your fault. We all knew the risk that comes with battle."

"You're back, m'Lord," Lorkan said, his relief obvious. "Please, m'Lord, don't run off like that again. I am responsible for your safety."

"You are right, Lorkan. And I apologize. I promise never to do it again."

Torgreth came strolling up, an impish grin curling the corners of his lips. "I told them you'd be back. Tried to get everyone to hide just to see the look on your face. Where's Bryok?"

"He's dead."

Torgreth's smile vanished.

Conal turned to Lorkan. "We need to meet up with Drustan and the others. What's our status here?"

"We're ready to move, m'Lord."

"Injured?"

"We lost eight killed, twenty-three wounded, two seriously. We've taken 156 prisoners. The rest are dead." He watched Conal glance around as if expecting someone. "He was one of the casualties, m'Lord," he gently informed him.

"Maldwic?"

"Yes, m'Lord."

Conal's shoulders slumped and his lips tightened. He had come to really like the man and knew he could count on him no matter the cost.

"Where's Seren?"

Lorkan hesitated. "They've left, m'Lord,"

"Left?" Conal stiffened, his nostril flaring.

"She said to tell you that they are not soldiers but highwaymen who only know how to steal and rob." His eyes softened. "Do not hold it against her, m'Lord. It is for the best. Maldwic was cut from a different cloth. He was a smart and loyal man who would obey without question. Yet he pushed his people beyond their level of comfort and abilities. Seren knows her limits. Still, she is loyal and will provide us with information regarding Tir Manach."

Conal grimaced and swiveled his head to glare at Torgreth. "I'm going to be mad at you if anything happens to you."

"Me too," Torgreth replied with a crooked grin. "How about we get going? I haven't seen that obnoxious brother of mine in far too long."

"We're ready to move out, m'Lord," Lorkan reminded him. "Bedo has your mount." He pointed back towards where the road curved around into the forest.

"Take charge, Commander." Conal stepped to the side to wait for Bedo.

They met up with Drustan and the dwarven army a day later just across the border into Gurim-duhr.

215

Drustan took the news especially hard that his brother was dead.

"I am sorry." Conal stood inside Drustan's tent, gazing tenderly at the druid whose whole body ached with a sadness beyond comprehension.

"What are we going to do?" Drustan muttered, shaking his head.

Conal cast a glance over his shoulder at the activity within the wide encampment spread out over the surrounding countryside. Together with Rorkyn's army, there were close to seven thousand dwarves and humans in a combined force. Lorkan and the dwarven king were in huddled planning when Conal excused himself to talk with Drustan.

Drustan looked up at Conal, his eyes moist. "Did he say anything to you?"

"He said something about Havengarde and giving it back and sacred and dragons' home, and none of it makes any sense to me. But I do know one thing... you are a dragon."

Drustan stiffened and shot a look past Conal to see if anyone heard. "Please keep that to yourself until I decide to reveal myself."

"Sure. Now explain to me what he meant." Conal scooted a field chair close to Drustan. "One thing I did notice was that anytime dragon hunters were close by, a rune on his arm would glow."

Drustan's eyes popped wide. "Dragon hunters? How many? Where?"

"We've eliminated them, at least all we know about," Conal reassured him.

Drustan flipped his arm over to glance down at the rune on his forearm. It was dark, revealing there were no dragon hunters close by.

"I swore to him that I'd protect you," Conal said, "but I need to know what I'm protecting. Tell me about Havengarde."

Drustan seated himself on the cot. "There was a time when dragons roamed freely. We lived in Havengarde and other locales, but Havengarde was our capital city, our refuge, our sacred place, for it was only in Havengarde that dragons could reproduce. I won't bore you with the history of why we dwelt in Havengarde, but know that we still hold the place sacred, especially now that our numbers have diminished to less than a dozen. If we cannot claim Havengarde again, then truly, dragons will cease to exist."

"How is that possible?" Conal argued. "Havengarde has been ruled by humans for hundreds of years."

"You forget how long dragons can live."

"OK, OK, point taken. But how did humans end up ruling Havengarde?"

Drustan exhaled a slow sigh. "Treachery. Dragons cannot work the earth like dwarves or humans. Our council met and decided to trust humans to build our refuge. It all seemed to be going well and we looked forward to the time when dragons would have their own city, a place sacred and holy where we could procreate. That lasted until almost the last stone was in place. Suddenly our friends became out captors, led by a man called Watcyn, a mason by trade, a wizard by reputation. The hunt for dragons began with him. Those who call themselves dragon hunters are bound by the same spells that that evil man created."

Drustan looked away for a moment then returned to his story. "Yes, dragons are powerful and in alliance with the right people would be quite the combination. But no one can fight everyone at once, for that is what happened. Humans and dwarves united to hunt us down."

"Not elves?"

Drustan shook his head. "No. Elves intuitively understand the balance in the world. It was because of the elves that we managed to save a remnant. It was the elves who discovered the runes of change that would allow us to appear in human form. Some of us called ourselves half-druids, because we were merely dragons in human form, albeit with the strength of dragons. Obviously we had to be careful, lest someone discover the truth."

"And there are eleven left now?"

"Yes. They are scattered throughout the kingdoms. With Bryok's death, there are five males and six females. But time is running out. Just like humans, there comes a point in a female's life when she is no longer able to reproduce. Two of our females have reached that age. It won't be long for the other four. If we do not reclaim Havengarde, you won't need dragon hunters anymore, for we will die of old age, never to rise again."

Conal stood and started pacing. "Did my father know all this?"

Drustan shrugged. "The story of dragons and Havengarde is lost to memory, except for dragons and those scholars who spend their days studying the arcane. I'm sure had your father known, he would have done something. Bryok and I had decided to trust him, but by the time we arrived in the city, Torian ruled."

He closed his eyes in reverie. "How odd it was to walk the streets of our city again. It had been over a hundred years the last time I was there. It took a while, but we found the home where we lived. It's all changed now. The building has been bricked in and apartments built in levels. It's a very fashionable part of the city now." He smiled. "I had to laugh at the stories developed over the years as to why the streets were so wide. One such fable had it that the streets had to be wide enough for a four-team carriage to turn around."

He opened his eyes and pierced Conal with an intense stare. "Will you keep your promise... or do I place my hope in another?"

"You know who I am," Conal evenly replied. "I will repeat the last words your brother spoke to me. He said that he knew I was the one... that he had known it from the beginning. Nothing's changed. We go to reclaim Havengarde... before it's too late for all of us."

THE END OF BOOK 2

Gwen and Conal's journey continues in

Empire of Serpents (available 12/15/20).

If you enjoyed the adventure so far, we'd love it if you left a review!

ABOUT THE AUTHORS

Richard Fierce

Hey there!

I write fantasy and space opera, and you can find all my books in many different eBook stores. You can check out my website for more information about my books, my next projects, and events I'll be attending where you can meet me and even get signed books.

Sign up here to find out when Richard releases new books!

WEBSITE

www.richardfierce.com

FANTASY

Dragon Riders of Osnen

Trial by Sorcery

A Bond of Flame

The Warrior's Call

The Coin of Souls

Wings of Terror

Eyes of Stone

The Fallen King Chronicles
Dragonsphere
The Fallen King
The Valiant King
The Restored King

Magic and Monsters
The Wizard and the Frog

Spellbreather Novels
Smoke and Blood

Anthologies
Chronicles of Mirstone

Standalone
Shard of the Sun

SPACE OPERA
Galactic Mercenaries
Steel for Hire
Steel for Free
Steel for All

pdmac

pdmac spent a career in the US Army before transitioning to education as a university Academic Dean. He transitioned again and now writes fulltime. He has a MA in Creative Writing and a Ph.D. in Theology. He is a member of the Blue Ridge Writers Guild, the Steampunk Writers and Artists Guild, and the Georgia Writers Association. A diverse author, writer, and editor, he has also edited a Literature anthology, served as managing editor of an archaeology magazine, ghost-written an autobiography, and has had poems, short stories, articles, and editorials published in various literary journals, magazines and newspapers. His most recent short stories appear in the *Short Story America* anthologies III and IV, *Poets in Hell*, *The Mulberry Fork Review*, and the Fantasy Anthology *Chronicles of Mirstone*. He has also sung back-up for Broadway plays, provided voice for radio plays, and acted and directed theater stage productions. In his off time, he and his wife race mountain bikes, kayak, and occasionally backpack sections of the Appalachian Trail. Additionally, he and his wife love to travel, their favorite place so far being Crete, Greece.

WEBSITE
www.pdmac-author.com

FACEBOOK
www.facebook.com/pdmacauthor/

Bridge Quest: A GameLit Adventure Series

Bridge Quest

Orc's Bane

Lord of Innis Torr

The Sci Fi/Fantasy Series Wolf 359:

Wolf 359

Queen to Play

A Once and Future King

The Puppet King

The Templar Rebellion

Wolf 359 – Box Set

Steampunk Western: Tombstone Series

Fool's Gold

An Ounce of Lead

The Devil's Disciple (Spring 2021)

Viking Time Travel Romance

Beyond Her Touch

A Dystopian Novel:

Rebirth of Angels

224

A Time Travel Novella

Ctrl Z: The Do Over Stone

Poetry

a young man no more